Basho thinks he knows all his mother's sins, since his mom is one sinister, mysterious figure. All his life she has been an overbearing figure he can't emulate, and each and every day, he feels he's failed her. Except now he's landed a top job in Tokyo, working for the sexy, compelling Kanji Chang, and Basho believes his fortunes have changed. But Kanji also has mysteries and often gives off a sinister air. And when the two men tumble into bed, Basho is surprised when Kanji actually bites him.

Though the bite leaves no telltale physical signs, Basho's whole body goes through changes. He can see and hear better. Sleep is a distant memory, and he has super-fast speed. He also views the world in a different way. But everything hurts, and noises are too loud, while his eyes begin acting weird.

And then things get even odder when Basho's mother descends for a visit and spills the family secret. Is she nuts, or is the family's closely guarded recipe for Stranger Rice not the only thing they hold dear? As Basho dreams of whiskers, he realizes his hot new lover sometimes has four legs, a tail, and a ferocious roar . . .

Stranger Rice

ISBN: 978-1-4874-3197-6
Cover art by Martine Jardin

Published by eXtasy Books Inc or
Devine Destinies, an imprint of eXtasy Books Inc

Look for us online at:
www.eXtasybooks.com or www.devinedestinies.com

Stranger Rice

By

A.J. Llewellyn and D.J. Manly

Dedication

Dedicated to the memory of all those beautiful animals, extinct, or in existence, that have been maimed, abused and killed by human hands. May we remember and stand up for those creatures and stop the abuse.

Chapter One

"Relax," the masseur whispered. "So tense."

Tense? Yeah, Basho Loy was tense. Try as he might, he couldn't let go of the persistent worry that he'd left something undone. Some small task in his over-filled day had not been completed.

He went over his mental to-do list. No, there was nothing, but still, he fretted.

Basho had been employed and extremely well paid for eleven months now. He worked an eighty-hour week most of the time, and fear and anxiety were his closest companions.

"Relaaaax." The masseur's voice was a ghostly whisper upon his very soul.

Basho loved these massages. He got one each and every Thursday night, the only way he could get through the toughest day of his job. Friday. And the only way he could really relax and persuade himself to stay away from the office on the weekends.

Still on his stomach, he gave in to Haku's thumb now pressing into the center of his right calf.

Basho stifled a scream. Ah. It hurt so good.

When Basho thought of everything he put his mind and body through each week, he wondered how he hadn't had a heart attack yet.

I'm only twenty-five, he reminded himself as shivery spirals of pain shot from his ankle bone, working their way up to the back of his knee.

"Breathe," Haku insisted.

Basho breathed. In spite of the soreness, he was becoming turned on. Haku kept up his gentle yet razor-sharp focus on points of Basho's body that Basho never knew were in agony until Haku applied the tiniest pressure. Basho could feel the heat rising in his groin. It swamped his senses with the mingled pain until he dutifully breathed in and out.

Haku was right. Breathing helped shift the burning sensation, helped in sending it off to the stratosphere. Where did all that intense pressure go? Haku worked on the left leg now. Basho knew the masseur would return to the right leg one more time, to make sure there was no more discomfort. Basho resisted falling asleep, although he needed it. Sleep was a waste of time in a massage. He had to stay awake, he needed to be aware of all the tender points and help move the ache away.

He could just make out the ambient street sounds over the Japanese lute music Haku played in his little studio. Basho didn't mind the faint noise. It made him feel alive. He spent his entire workweek in a gigantic tower, overlooking Hong Kong's business district, away from the streets.

Away from everything.

Ah. Haku pressed on the right calf again. Nothing. Then the left. Basho smiled into his buckwheat pillow. The legs were finished. That meant he could roll over and . . .

"Would you like a happy ending?" Haku asked.

He always asked, even though it was the part of the massage Basho craved most. Haku never rushed the happy ending. He wouldn't have dreamed of it, probably.

"Yes, please." Basho was no longer self-conscious when he rolled onto his back and his cock sprang into the air. He had begun to believe Haku would be offended if he didn't have a painful boner. It was just one more part of him that needed to *relaaaax*.

Basho inhaled the faint perfume of some floral oil. He

could never quite identify it, but its sense-memory lingered in his mind for days after a massage. Basho began to fantasize about coming here every evening. He could afford it, but was it a very decadent thing to do?

The idea both delighted and worried him.

Haku's warm hands began to work on Basho's groin, moving from side circles to the same relentless pressure on points that brought both pleasure and discomfort.

For some reason, each time Haku worked on this part of his body, Basho found himself transported to his childhood in Hungary. He usually saw images of walking along a dirt road with his grandfather. He hadn't thought of the old man for years, and yet here, he was crystal bright and very clear. Emotion welled in him.

He tried to think of other things. He twisted a little on the luxurious massage table, as if getting away from the precise fingertip pressure would ease the memories.

It would, but he was a glutton for punishment, apparently, because he always stayed until the very end. He almost cried out with joy when Haku's right hand began working up from the base of Basho's cock.

Haku had once told Basho that he was the most closed-off man he had ever met. "I wake your body up and you shut it down again. What happened to you that cut off your sexuality like this? It isn't healthy."

It had shocked Basho the first time Haku had spoken to him like this, but then Haku was a big, blond American who had embraced the Asian lifestyle and fashioned a lucrative career as a masseur in Hong Kong's new maze of gay bathhouses and karaoke bars on Hennessy Road.

The openly gay Haku had picked the right place to come to. His small studio high up in the business building called the Overseas Building had proved to be a goldmine. Hong Kong was still deeply closeted and so behind the times with regard to gay pride that the bathhouse scene and sex in public toilets were the rule rather than the exception.

Basho had been surprised to see so many otherwise elegant businessmen passing through places like the Wellington Street Public toilet and the men's sauna at the Mandarin Oriental Hotel. There were a few gay-friendly bars in the city, but Basho preferred the maze, as everyone called it. There were karaoke bars, Internet cafes. And Haku.

Haku and his maddening fingers of delicious doom.

The massage therapist released his grip on Basho's cock, which both calmed and frustrated Basho. He lay, eyes shut, waiting for Haku to pick up the oil bottle, and wasn't disappointed.

He wriggled at the squirting sound, which always seemed to harden Basho's cock all the more. He listened to Haku rubbing the oil onto his hands, and the smell of crushed flowers began to intoxicate Basho once more. Haku held one hand over Basho's nose, and with the other began to stroke him again. Basho smelled the flowery essence on the other man's hand and his mouth dropped open as Haku began pumping him, harder, faster, digging down to the base of Basho's cock. Just once he wished Haku would close his mouth around Basho's cockhead.

Basho could no longer open his eyes, nor could he contain his moans. He came with a yell, an eruption so deep and pure he saw nothing but whiskers of violet tendrils behind his eyes. A face loomed. It was always the same face he saw in these moments . . . Kanji Chang.

A white fire consumed his mind and spirit, and then Haku stroked his balls, applying pressure on the left one, which he somehow knew was more sensitive than the right. Basho thrashed under the steel-like grip that eked a fresh burst of semen from his body.

He fell back against the warm bedding, wishing the end

wasn't close. His eyelids fluttered as Haku covered him with a thick warm duvet, then moved down to his feet. He always ended the massage with the feet and head. This time, Basho had no choice. He fell asleep, aware of his own snoring but unable to stop it.

He had no idea how long he remained on the bed until Haku turned on a small lamp in the corner of the room. Basho was surprised to see that the room had been utterly dark. Night had fallen and the smiling Haku had brought him a cup of his favorite blend of tea—green tea with brown rice.

Haku raised the head of the massage table so that Basho could sit up and drink the hot liquid. Haku moved about the room slowly. The man was an artist, a saint, and a born healer.

"Don't rush," Haku insisted.

Don't worry, I won't. Basho simply smiled at the man and enjoyed the last few precious moments of their session. The tea was perfect. His whole body felt vibrant and at ease. By Monday night, he'd be tighter than hell again.

He half-watched Haku clean up the room then rose from the bed, taking his tea with him. He padded over to the tiny shower stall and set his cup on the edge of the sink. His clothes hung on the back of the door. He closed it then opened the shower taps, waiting for the water to warm. It didn't take long. Stepping into the pristine white tub, he gazed down at the city view from the small, open space between the frosted glass and the sill.

Basho could see straight down to the workmen's scaffolding on the front of the building. As he lathered the lemon soap onto his hands and began to wash, he watched people crossing the road. He knew the Hang Seng Bank on the ground floor of the building would be closed, as would the Bank of China next door.

The rest of the buildings had come to life though. Lights, action, secret assignations. He watched a couple running across the street hand in hand to the restaurant opposite Haku's building. He longed to hold hands with a lover. Longed for a man of his own, but doubted he would ever find one. Each gay man or *suspected* gay man he met was as closeted as he was. Besides, work was his life.

Fresh out of college twelve months ago, it had surprised him when the powers that be at Oumi Ocean International had thought he was the appropriate man to handle their entire marketing department.

Recruited right before his graduation day at Harvard, he'd been stunned but grateful. Very, very grateful when Kanji Chang, the company's chief executive officer, had personally called him on his cell phone and requested to interview him.

He'd been shocked at how young Kanji was. He said he was thirty, and he was drop dead gorgeous in a Chinese matinee idol kind of way. He wore his dark hair cut in a boyish style that fell over his dark brown eyes. There was something special about Kanji. It wasn't just his looks. He seemed older, more mature than most men Basho had met. And then there was his gait. It was the way he moved. Cat-like almost. He hardly ever smiled, not that Basho had ever seen, and seemed to constantly fight to contain himself. He gave off a feral heat that seemed at odds with his well-cut suits and calm demeanor.

Basho felt certain the man would be a tiger between the sheets.

They met in New York in the lobby bar at Kanji's hotel, and he'd been surprised when Kanji said, "I know your family is Chinese and that you were raised in Hungary until you were nine. That's when your mother sent you to relatives in San Marino, California, correct?"

"Yes," Basho had mumbled. Their appointment at five p.m. would normally dictate cocktails were in order, but Basho decided on the spot that the apparent investigation into his background meant he should stay alert.

He'd almost fallen off his chair when Kanji's next question was, "And I believe you can trace your family origins to the Han people."

Basho had been so shocked he couldn't respond. He'd squinted at the man who'd flown a long way to meet him and wondered why this was important. There were very few families who could trace their ancestry to the historically imposing Han Chinese, but yes, Basho's family could. And somehow his people had wound up in Hungary before moving to the US.

Kanji placed a lot of importance on Basho's background, saying the Hans were the most fearless and brilliant of all the Chinese.

"Is your family Han?" Basho had ventured. He'd picked up his glass of mineral water and the straw had gone right up his nose.

Suave, Basho, real classy.

He thought the interview would be over right there and then, but Kanji seemed a world away.

"My people are not Han, but I am fascinated by your race."

Before Basho could even contemplate what was so fascinating about the Han, Kanji offered him an outrageous sum of money to come to Hong Kong and work for him.

As Basho turned off the taps and dried himself, he marveled that with absolutely no experience, Kanji was convinced that Basho was the perfect man to handle Oumi Ocean International's marketing department.

Basho had spent little time in China or its environs. He'd grown up in Hungary, where, according to Kanji, many of the Hans had traveled to centuries ago. He had specifically referred to the name Loy and how many of them could be traced to Eastern Europe.

It had seemed odd then, and even more so now.

He loved Hong Kong, and his greatest fear was being fired. Everybody in the company feared it. He tried not to think about being out of work as he put his beautifully cut clothes back on, wishing his massage was only just beginning. He didn't want to leave. He wanted to stay here, feeling nurtured and tranquil, not hurried and frightened.

As the steam cleared from the mirror, Basho looked at his face and saw what everybody else could. He was a darkly handsome man, but . . .

He did not look Chinese.

All his life, once his family had sent him to the live in the US, he'd worried that not looking Asian would hamper his career. It had been hammered into him from high school that being Asian was his biggest asset.

The fascinating Hans had left their home for reasons unknown and assimilated into Eastern European society. Somehow Kanji had found him and pursued him.

Basho took a deep breath and straightened his tie.

He had to look perfect.

Oumi Ocean International was one of China's most successful producers of machinery in the western world. They made bulldozers and held a seventy-five percent stake in an Italian yachting manufacturing company. OOI designed and manufactured everything from commercial machineries like excavators, backhoe loaders, tractors, farm implements to small concrete mixers, castings, and more.

Fully dressed, he returned to the small massage space, where Haku was waiting for him. As usual he bowed deeply to Basho, who realized the next client must be waiting in the outer waiting room. Two men never ran into each other here, but Basho sensed the stranger's presence.

He peeled some Hong Kong dollars out of his wallet, including a handsome tip for Haku. Basho had one remaining red envelope in his coat pocket and reminded himself to buy more. It was one of the eccentricities he enjoyed most about the Chinese-owned island. Money was put into red envelopes for good luck, before exchanging hands.

As he passed the envelope to Haku he said, "I'll see you next week."

"I look forward to it," Haku responded. His big red lips almost made Basho sigh. He was handsome and sexy. Not Basho's type, not that he had a type really.

Kanji Chang's face loomed in his mind.

Yeah. He's my type all right, but he doesn't even notice me. The idea hurt so much it made him frown. No. He couldn't spoil the euphoria he now felt. It's a crush. Just a crush. And ever since I took the job he's never even looked at me.

There had been one tiny moment recently when he thought Kanji might have noticed Basho in a meeting. Basho had made a joke and Kanji laughed along with the others. In the eleven months he'd known him, it was the second time Basho had seen pleasure on his boss's face. Now he daydreamed constantly about making the man smile and laugh.

He slipped out of the studio and took the elevator to the ground floor. The nagging pain in his left shoulder had vanished and his cock felt light as a feather. As a rule he never masturbated. He saw it as being a waste of time. Besides, it usually made him fall asleep and he had to work late into the evenings.

But not tonight.

With new shipments leaving Hong Kong in the morning, he, like all the other department heads would be down at the dockyard early, supervising the week's cargo departures. It was a quirk of the company. They all had to be there, even though Basho worked in marketing.

He contemplated dinner. He was hungry now. He stood outside the Overseas Building and pondered his options. Somehow his reminiscences over the massage had triggered a taste for Mexican food. Living near east LA, albeit the posh end of it, he and his friends had often delved into the late night taco stands of the downtown area for tacos.

Basho's stomach gave a welcome lurch at the idea of going to the Brickhouse.

He grabbed a red taxi at the nearby stand. The driver groaned when he gave him his destination, the Lan Kwai Fong area.

"Traffic," he moaned, but Basho remained impassive. Red taxis charged more than any other company, so the driver would make money.

Seventeen minutes later, after ducking and weaving around the early evening crush, Basho leaned forward.

"Here," he said.

The driver screeched to a stop, and Basho handed him some money.

When he got out of the taxi, he raced down a tiny alleyway to the restaurant that bore no sign, but was already packed. He grabbed a stool at the counter, already salivating over the meal he planned to order. Rib-eye steak, Manchego cheese, tomato salsa, and cilantro tacos.

He ordered quickly, enjoying the noise of the tiny cafe. People stared at him as though he were taking up space. Solo diners were often treated this way in Hong Kong, but he wasn't taking up table space by eating at the counter, so he relaxed and ordered beet fries, as well as the tacos, and a margarita to wash down his meal.

Once his food arrived, Basho ate fast. Some people complained about the meat in the tacos here, but he loved it. Everything was good and hot and so tasty the meal didn't last long. He dithered over whether to order his favorite dessert of spicy chocolate fondant, but decided he'd been decadent enough for one week and paid his check. Outside, the line, or queue, as they called it here, for tables, snaked around the corner. People were used to queuing for everything in Hong Kong. He took his time strolling home, wondering how different the city had been before the Chinese took control of it back from the British.

Some people said it wasn't very different, that the British had imposed their courteous ways on the city. Others said it was very different, more open. He could believe that, but still loved the place.

He walked to his apartment on Elgin Street in the Soho district. His company had found the place for him and he loved the neighborhood. Populated by mostly Western business types, it had all kinds of bars and restaurants, and even a comedy club. Like many other buildings, his had commercial enterprises on the first few floors and residential space above it.

Basho wondered briefly what Kanji was doing this evening. The man never seemed to keep still. He was always traveling, always moving.

They never ran into each other away from work, and at the office, Basho felt like the invisible man.

When he got inside his apartment, all his plans to watch the news on TV, make coffee and do some work, evaporated.

He barely had time to remove his clothes before falling into bed and was fast asleep.

All he dreamed off were lovely hands massaging his body, floral oils with a haunting scent and his grandpa teaching him how to fry a potato on a stick.

Chapter Two

The next morning, he awoke early, terror filling his senses when he realized he had fallen asleep without setting his alarm.

Daylight. He shouldn't still be in bed when the sun was up. His whole body shook as he checked the time.

Five a.m.

Phew. My body clock is working. He resisted the urge to shoot out of bed and sank back against the pillows for a moment, allowing the panic to subside. He rose and walked to the kitchen where he boiled water in the kettle. He hurriedly showered and dressed in khakis and a work shirt, his uniform for Fridays.

He was back in the kitchen just as the kettle began to whistle and his house phone rang.

Basho checked the readout, surprised to see it was his mother calling from her home office in Taiwan. He took the call as he made his usual cup of instant coffee.

"Hello, son," she said.

She's probably forgotten which of us she called.

"It's Basho, Mom."

"I know who it is, foolish boy." Mudan Loy sounded pissed. It couldn't be helped. She'd mothered five sons and parceled each of them off to family and friends as she bounced from one marriage to another. Her youngest son, now aged six, was the only one who lived with her and the only one Basho really knew. He'd looked after the kid for the last year of his college term when he'd lived off campus and hired a nanny to care for Liang. He felt sorry for the kid, who was now in Taiwan being raised by an *amah,* a nanny.

Basho actually adored the little boy but tried not to think of him. His life in Hong Kong was not conducive to raising a child, sweet as Liang was.

He sighed. His mother had been a rich workingwoman as long as Basho could remember. Every so often, motherhood tugged at her cash-register-heart and she'd announce she was coming to visit.

"I'm coming there in two weeks," she said.

Oh, joy. "You coming for work?" he asked, sipping at his coffee.

"No. I'm coming to see my son. I thought I might also check on my businesses, of course. But I do want to see you, Basho. You disappointed me, not coming home for Christmas."

He rolled his eyes. Taiwan was not his home. And she'd gone on an Eastern European river cruise with her latest boyfriend. Liang had gone to stay with one of Basho's other brothers. That's why he hadn't gone home. He checked the time, wondering if he could squeeze in a second cup of coffee before heading to the docks.

The uncomfortable silence between them grew wider and deeper.

Mudan might have the Chinese name for peony, but she was no flower. Certainly no shrinking violet. She was the most successful Asian businesswoman in the world, one of the reasons Basho had suspected Kanji had sought him out. He respected his mother, one of the most formidable women in the hotel industry. She owned a chain of boutique hotels and restaurants in China, and was always looking for new opportunities.

"Are you cooking much these days?" she suddenly asked.

"What?" he wondered if he'd tuned out some important part of their conversation. "Why do you ask?" He couldn't remember the last time he'd cooked.

"I'm planning to stay with you, son."

"You and your boyfriend?"

"He's my husband. We got married New Year's Day."

"Congratulations." *I wonder how long this one will last.* Basho's father had died when Basho was a baby. Some kind of skiing accident, the details of which were sketchy, but he'd left Mudan wealthy and . . . angry. She'd abandoned Basho to his paternal grandparents and he would have been happy had she left him there.

Instead, he was forced to become the model son, the one by which she judged all her other unfortunate offspring.

"I'm looking forward to you meeting Hiroshi."

Hiroshi? That was a Japanese name, not that Basho cared, but his mother . . . she tended to veer toward handsome, younger Chinese men she could control.

"And, I am looking forward to a bowl of your utterly amazing stranger rice."

The words fell between them.

He almost hung up on her.

"How long will you be staying?" He was aware how weak and croaky his voice suddenly sounded.

"One week."

Oh, boy. She'd been threatening to do this since he'd moved here. She'd been promising they'd visit. In fact, he had met her—once—in Kowloon, where they'd had an unusual, rustic lunch of fish by the beach. Drizzled in camellia oil, it had been the most delicious thing he'd ever eaten in his life. She of course, had turned around and bought the tiny beach café and turned it into another of her boutique hotels.

He suddenly realized that was the scent of Haku's oil. Camellia flowers!

His mother said, "Basho, we'll have fun. I want to see your office and meet all your new friends." She paused. "And I want to meet this fabulous new girlfriend of yours!"

He thought his heart might stop.

Basho had no friends. There were a couple of guys he talked to at the office.

And he had Haku.

Oh, my God. She wants to meet my girlfriend. Why oh why did I tell her I had a girlfriend? And she wants me to make stranger rice. For my stranger stepfather.

He checked the time. He'd been on the phone so long he was now two minutes late for the journey to the docks.

The sea port of Hong Kong was one of the busiest in the world and the largest one servicing southern China. A company van transported the staff of OOI down to the Kwai Tsing Container Terminal. The ride time gave Basho plenty of time to absorb this new catastrophe in his life.

How could he drum up a girlfriend and cherished, adored friends in time for his mother's visit in two weeks?

He glanced beside him at Péng Cho, the head of the distribution department. He'd had drinks with Péng twice since they'd started working at OOI. The skinny man sat staring down into the work gloves adorning his hands. Basho know that Péng dreaded Fridays as much as he.

"You feel like maybe grabbing some dinner when we finish work?" Basho asked.

Péng looked up at him blinking. "It's the company dinner. Aren't you going?"

Basho was so shocked he didn't know how to respond. As though shocked himself, Péng lowered his gaze and resumed his careful study of his work gloves.

Looking out the window, Basho wondered when the dinner had been arranged and why he hadn't been invited.

For about the tenth time since his mother had called, he chided himself for all the foolish nonsense he'd told her.

The van stopped and they all disembarked. For a long, torturous four hours, they examined pallets and shipping crates as though they were experts. They were forced to help the longshoremen, who frankly seemed more annoyed than thrilled that a bunch of pansy-ass business executives showed up each week in apparent support of the real workers.

Basho felt especially sorry for Matilda Yang, who had the hardest time, not only with the physical work, but Kanji's constant criticisms. He seemed to really dislike the young woman who spearheaded the publicity department. She could never do anything right.

That and the fact that Basho had once spied Kanji in a bathhouse had convinced him Kanji was gay. But Kanji wasn't here today, and Basho helped Matilda when he could.

"Thank you," she said, looking on the verge of tears.

Like Basho and Péng, she'd been recruited straight out of college. She'd graduated Summa Cum Laude from Yale, plucked apparently right out of the receiving line by Kanji and recruited for OOI before she'd even had time to think.

Kanji didn't seem to like the woman, but she never showed her distress. Basho knew she took it hard though. They worked longer and later than anybody else and he sometimes heard her crying softly in her office. He had no idea why Kanji targeted her. He was especially cruel on Fridays. Basho wondered at his boss's wisdom in forcing her down here. She was no Stevedore. None of them were. But still, they came and worked a full day.

And Kanji, when he made it down here, did what he did best. He supervised.

As they worked, Basho's agonies were allowed full bloom. He began to fret deeply about his imaginary girlfriend. For some stupid reason he'd told his mother his fictional goddess was named Matilda. He hadn't said she was his co-worker but it was an unusual enough name that she'd put two and two together and his lie would slap him in the face.

He couldn't introduce her to his mother. He just couldn't.

I'll email her and tell her we broke up. Why the hell did I make up all that stuff? Isn't it enough that I am a successful businessman?

No, it wasn't. He knew that. His mother held her sons to exacting, high standards and now his success was the blunt instrument with which she punished her other sons.

I have no other choice. I'll email Mom and tell her we broke up. I'll act all cut up about it so she doesn't ask too many questions.

With his plan of action formed in his mind, he was in better spirits when they broke for lunch. OOI's executives joined the throng crossing the busy shipyards to purchase noodle bowls at a nearby street stall frequented by many of the dockworkers. They waited patiently in line, the best part of the day in Basho's opinion, and he ordered the beef noodle soup. It came neatly packaged in a carton. He, Péng, and Matilda, sat on a load of unmarked pallets and devoured their simple meals.

Basho spooned the first flavor-burst of curried broth and beef into his mouth, savoring the tart taste of plum and crisp, green onion. The beef was so succulent and rich it warmed his whole body from the toes up. The thin egg noodles were just chewy enough to make the soup substantial.

"I needed that." Matilda stared up at the sky. "I'm thinking of making a job change," she whispered.

Both Basho and Péng stopped eating.

Basho almost swallowed his spoon. "What do you mean, change?" His spirits soared for the first time since Haku had massaged him. If she left town, this would be the perfect excuse.

"Change?" Péng echoed.

She nodded, a small glimmer of amusement in her eyes. "I'm thinking Starbucks."

At their incredulous expressions, she said, "Why not? Lots of college graduates end up there. And I make a killer espresso."

"But they just got busted for brewing coffee with toilet water," Péng said.

"I was joking," Matilda rushed to soothe him. "Half joking, anyway."

Neither man laughed. Basho's spirits had flopped again. How could he keep his mother out of the office and away from Matilda?

"I can't imagine ever buying coffee from that place again. Not after what I read in the *Apple Daily*." Péng seemed obsessed with Starbucks and its toilet water. "The Starbucks in the financial district—you know the one in the Bank of China building—"

Basho almost stopped breathing. That was the building next door to Haku's studio.

"It wasn't toilet water. They used water from a faucet in the parking garage," Matilda said, sounding agitated.

"Still creepy," Péng insisted. Basho was inclined to agree. His stomach roiled at the mere thought of it.

"Loafing again, Matilda?" a low, chuckling voice interrupted their discussion.

Matilda turned chalk white and hurried away from her companions.

Basho stared at Kanji, who'd just turned up and had an odd smile on his face.

The tiger who smiled.

Basho shook off the notion as their boss flicked a glance from Péng to Basho and strode off, muttering into his cell phone.

"That man totally hates us," Péng whimpered.

Basho swallowed hard. Yeah, he felt that way himself. The truth of his existence was a long way from his fantasies of wild sex with Kanji and a social life filled with dinner parties and karaoke nights.

Karaoke? When was the last time he'd sung? Back in the States, about a thousand years ago. He jumped off his perch, tossed the remnants of his lunch, and got back to work. As he slid on his work gloves, his cell phone rang. He checked the readout.

We're bringing Liang. You may need to invest in a rollaway, his mother had texted.

Oh, joy. He loved Liang but three visitors scrutinizing his life was more than he could bear right now. He got back to work pondering everything he'd need to do, which involved a lot more than investing in a rollaway before his visitors arrived.

He heard a burst of laughter and caught a glimpse of Kanji and Péng enjoying some joke. He realized that Kanji's hair had grown out a little, the ends kissing his collar. Basho's spirits plummeted to his shoes. Great. That was another thing. Basho hadn't been invited to the company dinner that evening.

Is he getting ready to fire me?

The thought lingered for the rest of the day until their containers were ready to ship. Basho hobbled back into the van with the other department heads, thankful he didn't need to go home and figure out what to wear that night.

He tried to shut his ears to the chatter among the others. He couldn't help overhearing that they were to dine at Above & Beyond, one of the hottest restaurants in Hong Kong. Basho had never been there. He'd read lots of reviews of the place and longed to try the food at the British-Cantonese restaurant overlooking Victoria Harbour, but the few clients he entertained on his expense account preferred cocktails and French food.

Back home, he took a long, hot shower and began to fret

anew about his family's visit. He dried off, changed into jeans and a T-shirt and headed to the kitchen. It was his favorite room in the house, even though he barely used it. He loved the two chef's ovens and the six-burner range lining one wall. On the other side, a double sink, dishwasher and ample cupboard space mocked him. He had nothing, save for a few glasses and a spoon.

In the center of the kitchen stood an island with an antique butcher's block, small sink and four-burner stove. It had storage cupboard and drawers and a breakfast bar in front of it with stools, where all his imaginary guests could talk to him as he prepared . . . boiled water.

He opened the cupboards, hoping beyond hope that some Hong Kong kitchen fairies had showed up since the last time he'd done some shopping and equipped him with adequate dishes and glasses.

No such luck.

He had one set of four drinking glasses and three coffee cups, having broken one. Awesome. He was a total loser for sure. He'd purchased these the day he moved in. He'd even bought a couple of spoons but somehow had managed to lose one.

Basho made a rough list on his iPhone and left the apartment, making his way to Wing On, a department store that specialized in home wares. The place was packed with mostly foreigners all exhibiting the same stress and worry he felt. He began to feel he should grab everything in sight, in case every item around him grew legs and vanished.

In short order, he'd picked up an eight-piece Western dinner service, a collection of Asian bowls, plates, serving spoons, Western flatware, glasses, chef knives, some pots and pans and kitchen appliances such as a rice cooker, a proper coffee maker, toaster, blender, and two cutting boards.

He pressed on to the soft furnishings section, buying

sheets, towels and two new duvets. He didn't need a rollaway for Liang. His little brother would sleep in the tiny den on the sofa that opened into a bed. Basho would give his mother and her new husband his bedroom and he himself would sleep on the living room sofa.

The living room. Ugh.

He'd need to buy an extra TV. Maybe two. Liang was addicted to *Spongebob Squarepants* and his mother was hooked on CNN. He bought two new flat screen TVs, taking advantage of a special travelers' sale by flashing his American passport. He then arranged to have everything delivered to his apartment the following morning.

Basho strolled out the front door, realizing he'd need to do some food shopping next, but really not feeling in the mood for it. Tomorrow he'd hit the Great supermarket and stock up on pantry items and, he realized, he'd need to practice his stranger rice. He hadn't cooked his family's specialty noodle bowl since he'd started college.

Famished now, he checked his watch. Almost eight o'clock. He was one of the few people who wore a watch. It was an old habit and one he wasn't likely to change anytime soon. Feeling good about being one step closer to being a good host, he wandered down the street and caught a taxi, heading to the Lan Kwai Fong district once again. His cell phone rang, but he ignored it. He recognized the song he had assigned his mother's phone number. He didn't want to ruin his appetite by getting bad news. Whatever it was, it could wait.

Near the High Street, he asked the driver to stop.

"Thank you," the man said, clearly not wanting to negotiate the tiny, four-hundred-foot street with so many people milling about.

Basho paid him and darted down to the tiny restaurant cheerfully lit from within. He peered through the windows at the packed tables. He'd been crazy to think he might nab one so late.

He was surprised when somebody from a corner table waved at him. Narrowing his eyes he looked closer, astonished to see Haku smiling at him.

Haku beckoned him inside. As Basho walked in, Haku jumped up to greet him. "Care to join us?" He indicated the man who had obviously been sitting with him and who sat beaming at Basho now from a table for two. "Or do you have a reservation?" Haku put his hand on Basho's shoulder.

Basho shook his head. "No, I don't. But I'm intruding."

"No, you're not. I'm glad to see you here. You're the one who turned me onto this place."

Haku led him to the small table. A waiter scurried over with a chair and a wine glass. Before he knew it, Basho had company for dinner, and a very nice Pinot Noir in his grip.

"Basho, I'd like you to meet my partner, John."

John was a handsome Asian man who extended his hand. They shook, perhaps a little too long, Basho feeling a little stunned to be embraced so warmly by Haku and his mate.

Dumfounded to see his massage therapist away from his studio, Basho felt tongue-tied, but the other men had no trouble chatting away. Haku looked just the same, his blond hair tied back in a black elastic band.

The wait staff obviously adored Haku and John. Everybody doted on them in a way none of them ever had with Basho.

"Are you very hungry?" Haku asked. "The lamb chop and homemade gnocchi are excellent."

"Sounds great to me." Basho smiled at the waiter, who scurried away and returned several minutes later with the most succulent meal Basho could ever remember eating. The lamb chop had been cooked to perfection. He savored every bite.

Haku and John were excellent dinner companions. They

chatted about everyday things with Basho, asking his opinion on all kinds of subjects. They laughed about Starbucks and its toilet water episode.

For Basho, it was such a relief not to talk about work, he was worried he would bore Haku and John. They laughed at his jokes however, and when the conversation turned to the mysterious Big Yellow Duck—as the Chinese bloggers called it—Basho was grateful he'd read about it online in between meetings.

The enormous, fifty-four foot duck had appeared in Victoria Harbour, much to the locals' amusement. But after a couple of weeks of providing pleasure to Hong Kong's residents, it had begun to disintegrate and sink. People pointed fingers, but so far no culprit could be found for the demise of the funny creature.

"Who do you think did it?" Haku's eyes danced with amusement as he refilled Basho's wineglass.

"I'm going with the bird flu theory," Basho said, making Haku and John laugh. Bird flu was the other big topic of discussion in Hong Kong with its ever-present threat.

Emboldened by their enjoyment of his joke, Basho added, "He should have drunk some *ban lan gen.*"

More laughter. *Ban lan gen* was a medicinal root well known in Chinese communities to ward off virus and fever. People usually drank it as tea. Suddenly, the image of a plastic duck drinking a cup of tea made Basho laugh long and loud. He couldn't remember the last time he'd had such a good time.

"Have some dessert," Haku said. "Have you tried the English soup?"

Basho shook his head. He'd seen it on the menu but had never actually eaten it. The specialty of the house turned out to be a kind of decadent English trifle with warm custard, chocolate, and a creamy topping. Basho moaned as he scraped the last of the sherry cake off the plate.

"That was so much fun," Haku said, swiping the check before Basho could stop him.

"My treat next time," he insisted.

Haku bowed to him. "It would be our pleasure."

Next time. Maybe he could ask Haku and John to dine with him when his mother was in town. There was no need for her to know that Haku gave him massages. The man was sweet, intelligent and great company.

Swallowing the last sip of wine, he followed Haku and John outside. They stood so close to one another it seemed obvious they were lovers. They took turns hugging Basho, thanking him for a wonderful evening and with that, they held hands and disappeared into the night.

Basho envied their openness, their genuine pleasure in one another. Would he ever find a love of his own?

He walked home in a pleasing whirl that only a good meal, slight drunkenness and great conversation could produce. Exhaustion didn't hit him until he went into his apartment and switched on the living room lights. He kicked off his shoes, switched on the TV and curled up on the sofa. He was just in time to catch a news report that the Big Yellow Duck would be saved. He'd apparently been dented by the waves in the harbour. Poor Duck!

Basho laughed into his cushions now propped under his head. He fell asleep as a grave-faced official assured the Hong Kong public that their favorite duck was safe.

He slept oddly, dreaming inexplicably of wild tigers and . . . stranger rice. He tossed and turned, Kanji's face looming in his mind, that wicked, sexy smile on his face.

"I love stranger rice," Kanji said in the dream. "How do you make it?"

Basho smiled in the dream. Kanji was in his kitchen,

standing at the breakfast bar with a wineglass in his hand.

What's he doing in my kitchen? Basho fretted but the dream wouldn't leave his mind.

"What kind of meat are you using?" Kanji asked, smiling at Basho over the rim of his glass. "I know when one is serving stranger rice to a visitor, one is supposed to serve the finest cut of meat possible."

"I'm using lamb." It had been fixated in Basho's mind since the moment he sampled the mouth-watering chop over dinner.

"Lamb isn't bad. Have you ever tried cooking it with human meat?"

Basho sat up on the sofa, sweating. He looked around, the place was in darkness. At some point he must have powered off the remote.

Human meat. What a weird dream. As if his boss were some kind of cannibal! Sheesh . . .

His pulse raced, his heart thumped. Taking deep breaths, he checked the time on the DVD player. It was a quarter to five in the morning. He rose from the sofa, focusing on trying to still his shaking limbs and went to the kitchen for water.

Basho was shocked to find a wineglass sitting on the countertop. What the . . .

He picked it up. It resembled one of set he'd bought the night before but he'd asked for them all to be delivered. He twisted the stem in his fingers.

How weird.

Basho slid the glass into the cupboard with the few tumblers he had in there, then tore a page off the magnetic note pad he kept on the fridge door.

No longer wanting water, Basho found a pen in his utility drawer and began making a list of all the food he'd need to buy. Top of the list were the ingredients he'd need for stranger rice. His grandpa in Hungary had been the one to teach him about it. He'd explained that as a child, he had lived in China, where even the poorest families needed to prepare food for visitors. Stranger rice, which was a delicious blend of broth, rice and rich meat, was a nutritious, filling meal-bowl that was inexpensive to prepare, save for the cut of meat. That didn't have to be a huge piece, but the best one could buy. Grandpa had taught him to buy the best, prime beef he could afford. If he spotted tenderloin, ribeye or strip steak on sale, he'd snap it up and freeze it for future use.

Stranger rice was a tradition not practiced in many other families Basho knew, yet all his friends clamored for this meal. He'd been making his own since he was ten years old.

It seemed weird now that it had been so long since he'd cooked. He also noted to buy fresh ground coffee. His mother would be appalled to learn he'd been drinking instant, standing over his kitchen sink swallowing it in great gulps before work each day.

He finished his list, then showered, letting the hot water spray hit his back, ironing out the kinks.

By the time he left his apartment at six o'clock, morning had broken like a pale pink egg over fluffy marshmallows. Sunrise was breathtaking. He hurried to his favorite collection of street stalls at Kowloon Market, where the most dazzling array of fruits and vegetables could be found. The exterior of the market looked like a capsized cruise ship.

Basho raced from one stall to the next loading up on things he thought he could store in the fridge and freezer.

At the Great supermarket, he bought lamb chops, trying not to think about his strange dream. He bought several cuts of meat, a bag of rice, tons of noodles, spices and condiments. As an afterthought he picked up a bag of whole bean coffee, reminding himself to buy a French press.

With an hour to spare before his new home wares arrived,

he dropped in on the One-Eyed Man's Cooling Tea stall for a reviving cup of *leung cha*. The mysterious blend of herbs and tea known to cure everything, was the obsession of most working people in Hong Kong. He'd started shopping at the right time. The crowds were streaming into the markets and stores now, long queues forming.

He sipped his tea, feeling much better now.

Except my thoughts of Kanji. Why am I even thinking about the guy? He didn't even invite me to the company dinner!

He bought a couple of bags of *leung cha* from the stall holder. He needed to stop. After all, he didn't even have a teapot. Back out on the street, the air felt pleasingly soft and warm. He found a taxi and headed home, his fingers hurting from the many bags laden with his purchases.

Once inside his apartment, he raced to the kitchen, dropping his bags on the counter with relief.

He took a deep breath before unpacking and storing the food. He had a sudden, inexplicable feeling of doom that he couldn't explain.

I'm just hungry, that's all.

He shook off the odd, scary sensation and began stowing his new purchases. Within minutes, the intercom buzzed. He didn't recognize the sound at first because he couldn't remember the last time he'd had a visitor.

The caller's voice crackled and popped. It was the delivery guy with his new stuff.

Basho let him in, and within minutes the hallway was crammed. Basho gave the man a tip when the final items were settled on the ground and he closed the front door.

With shaky hands he sought the bags around him for the wine glasses he'd bought.

The first set was full. He opened the second.

One glass was missing.

But he knew where it was. Inexplicably it was on the shelf inside his kitchen cupboard.

Chapter Three

Basho dropped to the ground staring into the box. There had to be some explanation. Had he been drunk the night before when he shopped? No. He shook his head. How . . . weird. He sat there a long time, deciding he must have brought the glass home. He was stressed out. Yes, that was it. He was stressed out and had no idea what he was doing. He'd taken the glass out for some reason and brought it home.

I need to work less. I need to relaaax more. Yes. That's what I need to do. I need to get two massages a week. That will help.

He got to his feet, determined to put the incident behind him. He dragged the TVs to their respective rooms, then unpacked and washed all his new dishes. He found homes for his new cookware and the chef knives. His kitchen was beginning to look lived-in. He liked it.

Basho was starving. He'd missed breakfast, but since it was now eleven o'clock, it was close to lunchtime so he might as well make some stranger rice.

He raced to his bedroom, bringing his iPod dock and long-ignored iPod into the kitchen and plugged it in. He flipped through his music choices and chose The Carpenters. *Superstar* was one of his favorite songs. He'd always performed it in the karaoke clubs back in New York.

Don't you remember you told me you loved me baby? He sang along with the brother-sister duo as he began to prepare his simple but hearty dish, working at the kitchen island. He began with the sauce, making his own sea stock, or *dashi*, out of *kombu*—dried kelp flakes, which he boiled in water. He turned off the heat and added *katsuobushi*—dried tuna—and let it steep. The longer he kept the blend stored, the better. He used half for his soup and put the rest in a glass in the fridge. That was something else he needed to buy. Storage containers.

He boiled his rice, then turned to the rest of his sauce, a potent blend of mirin—Japanese rice wine—soy sauce, his homemade *dashi* and sugar. He sang as he worked, his grandpa's voice echoing in his mind. "Cook with love, Basho. Cook with love and everything you present on a plate will have been made with your whole heart."

Grandpa had been the first one to explain to him that a meal must consist of the five basic tastes: sweet, sour, salty, bitter, and *umami*. Umami was the epitome of meatiness, fundamental to all Eastern cuisine.

His stranger rice came back to him as if no time had passed since he'd last prepared it. He seasoned his lamb, leaving it to marinate in a blend of spices and chopped onion.

This meal would be perfect with a glass of red wine. His mind flew to the dream he'd had of Kanji in his kitchen. Yeah, like that'll ever happen.

His intercom buzzed. How odd. Had the delivery guy forgotten something? He was surprised to hear his boss's voice.

"It's me," Kanji said.

"Me?" Basho asked, but he knew who it was. He flew into a state of instant panic as Kanji growled.

"Let me in," he demanded.

Basho dutifully pressed the buzzer, dismayed when his fervent prayer to the gods and goddesses of workers everywhere to open the ground and swallow him up went ignored.

He had several alarming minutes before the elevator arrived during which he had ample time to freak himself out completely. Was Kanji coming here to fire him? Visions of security guards stripping him of his office key cards and laptop danced in his head.

The elevator doors pinged open and his fear peaked as Kanji stepped out, looking as immaculate and unattainable as ever. His dark hair gleamed as he strode toward Basho. He was alone, so maybe things weren't as bad as Basho thought.

"Hi." Basho waved, feeling like a simpleton.

A small smile curved its way onto Kanji's mouth. "You look well enough," he said. "So I assume you have some very good reason for missing dinner last night."

Basho's mouth fell open. For some odd reason the first thing that popped into his head was Mary Poppins telling her tiny charge, "Close your mouth, Michael. We are not a codfish."

"Last night?" he echoed feebly as Kanji walked right past him into the apartment, his head swiveling in every direction.

Basho closed the door, realizing he'd left his sauce bubbling on the stove. He hurried to the kitchen, but Kanji lingered in the living room. Basho stood, holding the sizzling pan, wondering what his boss was doing.

Kanji finally entered, his see-all gaze taking everything in.

"Your home is not what I expected."

Basho's hand shook from sheer nerves. "What were you expecting?" He placed the pan back on the stove so he didn't slosh boiling hot liquid all over himself. He tipped the marinating lamb into the pan.

"Well, I thought you'd live a far more . . . Spartan lifestyle. I didn't think your space would be quite so . . . cluttered."

Cluttered? Up until this morning it wasn't. Basho's heart sank.

"So, why did you skip dinner last night?"

Basho glanced down at his pan. "I didn't skip it. I wasn't invited."

"That's ridiculous." I sent out emails to everybody last

Monday."

"Well, I didn't get one." Basho quickly spooned sauce over the lamb chop. It was coming along nicely. Oh, God. Why was he still cooking? He was about to get the um, chop.

Kanji began rifling through his cell phone. He flicked a glance at Basho. "What are you making?"

"Stranger rice."

"I love stranger rice," Kanji said, just like he had in the dream. A chill ran down Basho's neck. Kanji leaned over the breakfast bar, staring down at the stove. "How do you make it?"

Basho smiled, also like he had in the dream, except Kanji didn't have a wineglass in his hand.

What's he doing in my kitchen? Basho fretted just like he had in the dream. If he mentions human meat I'm jumping out the window.

"Do you have any wine?" Kanji suddenly asked.

"No." Basho shook his head. "Sorry." He flicked a glance at the oven clock. Twelve noon. He felt like a character in the movie *Shane*. He was about to enter a battle of wills. Without the guns.

"Really?" Kanji shocked Basho by opening a cupboard. There stood three bottles of wine Basho had never seen before. He almost giggled.

"Oh, look what I found." Kanji brought down a bottle. "Pinot Noir. My favorite."

He came to stand beside Basho, nudging him aside a little. He opened a drawer and took out a bottle opener, which Basho had also never seen in his life. He just kept staring at his boss, who popped open the wine.

"How rude of me," Kanji said. "Would you like a glass?"

Basho shook his head. Kanji poured himself a glass and moved back to the other side of the breakfast bar.

"What kind of meat are you using?" he asked, smiling at

Basho over the rim of his glass. "I know when one is serving stranger rice to a visitor, one is supposed to serve the finest cut of meat possible."

Oh. My. God. It's just like the dream. This can't be happening.

"I'm using lamb." He hid his trembling hands in his pocket, awaiting with dread his employer's response.

Kanji nodded and sipped. "Lamb isn't bad. Have you ever tried cooking it with pork loin?"

"I have some in the freezer." Basho felt weak. He wished Kanji would go ahead and fire him or tell him why he was here. He passed a hand across his eyes, trying not to think about the three bottles of wine in the cupboard. He was getting a headache now.

"Basho, I'm sorry," Kanji suddenly said.

"You're—"

Kanji held up his cell phone, a rueful expression on his face. "You're absolutely right. Somehow your email address was left off the macro on the Excel spreadsheet. You weren't invited." He looked surprised.

Basho didn't know how to respond. Did he say, that's okay, or should he say nothing?

He became aware of Kanji's stare.

"Did you worry when you weren't invited?"

Basho turned off the stove. "Of course." He had two choices. Invite the man to lunch or let the most perfect meal he'd ever cooked go to waste.

"I hope you're inviting me to lunch," Kanji said.

"Of course," Basho said again. He dished the food into bowls, setting them onto plates with serving spoons beside them, realizing he'd neglected to buy chopsticks. He bit his lip.

"Problem?" Kanji asked, peering over the breakfast bar.

"I don't have chopsticks."

"Yes, you do." Kanji came and stood beside him again, rummaging through drawers, as Basho looked on, wondering if his boss turned up at all his employees' homes and invited himself to lunch.

"Only the cute ones." Kanji seemed to be reading his mind. Why not? It went along with every other weird thing that had happened to him since he'd woken up this morning.

Wait. Did he just say I was cute?

Kanji produced two sets of antique-looking red lacquered chopsticks Basho had definitely never seen before. He swallowed hard as Kanji nudged the drawer shut with his hip.

He glanced at Basho. "These were probably left by the previous tenant."

Maybe that explained it. Basho worked hard to tamp down his mounting panic. He was certain he'd looked through all the drawers when making his shopping list. His head was stuck on *only the cute ones*.

"You like eating this way?" Kanji asked.

"Hmm?" Basho looked up from his bowl. He'd dipped his spoon into the broth and had swallowed a mouthful without even realizing it. "Usually." He smothered a smile.

Kanji leaned into him, his wonderful, spicy, but delicate aftershave packing a pungent wallop to Basho's senses as he deposited a kiss on Basho's cheek.

"You *are* cute," he said.

Basho almost dropped his bowl. One minute, he thought his boss was going to give him the chop, the next, Kanji was kissing him.

"Every successful seduction begins with an unexpected move," Kanji said.

"What did you say?" Basho was certain he hadn't heard right.

"I said you're cute. You want to eat at the dining table?"

Basho nodded, unable to speak. Had he imagined Kanji's

words? No, he didn't think he had, but he couldn't explain them any more than he could explain the wine glass mystery, the chopsticks, or—

Successful seduction. No, Basho hadn't fantasized that. Or was he going crazy? As far as he knew there was no history of insanity in his family. Perhaps it had skipped a few generations. He followed Kanji into the dining room, where they sat side-by-side, Kanji eating with impeccable manners. Everything he did was so damned sexy.

"I don't think I've ever tasted anything so wonderful," Kanji said, clearly enjoying every bite. "I didn't think I'd enjoy the lamb but it's perfect. Absolutely perfect." He glanced at Basho's bowl and frowned. "I know you're hungry, why aren't you eating?"

Basho picked up his spoon again. "I get nervous around you," he admitted. He wasn't sure if this was a smart thing to do, but for him, it was the truth. He couldn't act all suave and sophisticated when he was afraid, so afraid he thought he might pee his pants.

Kanji set his chopsticks across the top of his bowl and looked at Basho beside him. "Did you think I was coming here to fire you today?"

"Yes." Basho shrugged. "You sounded really pissed."

"I was." Kanji stared into his half-empty bowl. "You cook with love. Did you know that?"

Something in the man's gaze broke Basho's heart. He bit his lip again. His emotions whirled, his brain could think up any good response.

"I've watched you for a long time." Kanji's voice seemed to come from some long, dark tunnel.

Basho felt feverish. He was in some kind of dream. Kanji left the table and returned with the wine bottle and an extra glass.

"Wine brings out the flavor of your delicate cooking,"

Kanji said, pouring some for Basho. He slid it toward him and sat down again. Basho sipped. Somehow it was easier than trying to eat. The wine was very good. Smooth, buttery—

"Here, Basho. Try a little lamb. Come on, open your mouth." Kanji held a piece of meat with his chopsticks, pressing it toward Basho's lips.

Basho opened and inhaled the morsel. It was the best meat he'd ever cooked.

Kanji moved closer and kept feeding Basho from his own bowl. Basho kept eating, bewildered, yet more turned on than he'd ever been in his life. He was aware of his own breathing, of every single beautiful dark lash accentuating Kanji's eyes. He was so cat-like. Lithe, mysterious, oozing manliness. It made Basho think of a tiger in the jungle hunting prey.

No.

Not prey.

A mate.

He wants me. Oh God. I feel it now. Why? Basho's thoughts began to spin as he sipped his wine again, at Kanji's coaxing. He swallowed, then gasped when Kanji began nuzzling him with tiny kisses. They rained across his chin and cheeks, finding a welcome home on Basho's waiting mouth. He was in a dream, a beautiful, sexy, frightening dream. He never wanted to awaken, he'd longed for this man for so long.

And then the kisses reached the pulse point in his throat and Basho could no longer think straight. He and Kanji reached for each other at the exact same moment.

"Bedroom?" Kanji asked. Basho couldn't speak. He pointed over his shoulder.

With a low growl, Kanji took Basho by the hand and led the way.

Basho prayed that nothing would stop what was about to happen, but once they reached his room, fear overtook him again. He was inexperienced and knew it, but it didn't seem to matter. Kanji reached for him with tender kisses that soon turned fierce.

They tore at each other's clothes. Basho wanted to remember each second of this, but time moved so fast. He could hear his sounds of desire, of sheer need, echoing in Kanji's throat, and as the other man reached for Basho's now-exposed cock, they were fully evident.

"This is a nice surprise." Kanji's voice was a low growl. He pushed Basho to the bed, their gazes locking. Basho stared up into the large eyes that now looked flecked with amber. There was nothing gentle or elegant about the way Kanji tugged off Basho's shoes and pants. He knelt on the floor between Kanji's parted thighs, sucking his cock with untamed lust. Basho lifted his head when he felt something sharp. He thought he spotted claws on Kanji's fingers and closed his eyes.

I've got to stop drinking wine. When he opened them again, there were no claws.

Basho's head fell back against the bed. I'm going crazy. He's doing things to me nobody has ever done to me before.

Kanji opened Basho's legs wider, pushing them up to Basho's chest.

Please. Oh, please. Don't stop.

For a long moment Kanji did nothing. Basho lifted his head again and looked down. No mistaking the predatory gleam in the man's eyes as he studied Basho's cock and balls.

"What a nice surprise," he said again. Kanji's voice was so low and so seductive, Basho almost came on the spot. Kanji began licking him in such a slow, deliberate way it stoked a deep fire within Basho. He twisted and turned on the bed, unseen flames licking at him from within. He came in Kanji's mouth, shocked at the sweet sensation of erupting in a warm, wanting mouth.

Kanji didn't stop. He licked Basho like a cat might, starting from Basho's ass, up to his balls and back to his cock again.

Basho fell back against the bed once more, surprised at the rough sensation of Kanji's tongue. He opened his eyes and glanced down, but the other man's tongue went back to feeling smooth.

I'm not used to all this attention. Basho reached out for Kanji, his fingers sinking into the man's silken hair. Kanji murmured, "Can't wait," and stood, flinging off his own pants and shoes.

His cock was gorgeous. Neither man had what Basho would have described as an Asian cock. Kanji was plenty well endowed. Basho longed to suck him but Kanji seemed consumed with fucking him.

Basho would have suggested a rubber, but had none. No. He couldn't stop it now. He had to have Kanji. He needed and wanted him so much.

Kanji pushed Basho up farther on the bed, climbed on top of him and covered his body with his. Basho let his hands roam the other man's taut, muscular back and shoulders. Kanji moved down again, taking his time to lick Basho's asshole.

Basho moaned as Kanji lapped at him, preparing Basho for the huge cock that he then took in hand, rubbing against the crack.

Basho moaned. He loved that Kanji didn't rush things, but that fire in Basho's cock was back to full heat now and he was sweating.

Kanji rubbed the head against the hole. Basho moved back and forth, trying to get the man inside him. The head slipped in. The pain of the welcome intrusion momentarily blinded Basho. Just as he thought he couldn't tolerate the agony, Kanji moved a little deeper into him, kissing him again. He began biting Basho's neck.

Basho had enjoyed hickies in his youth but began to worry.

The bites were not only painful, but he worried about how he'd cover them up at work. They distracted Basho from the searing ache in his ass, and then . . . bliss.

Kanji sucked on his throat harder now, but the throbbing turned to waves of pleasure that shot straight through his body. Kanji was inside him, fucking him with a relentless stroking that inflamed both of them.

Basho cried out, "More!" and Kanji bit him again.

They came together, fire-on-fire, and Basho had the strange thought. *Nothing will be the same.*

Kanji fell on top of him.

Basho kissed his cheek and mouth, Kanji returning his embrace.

Kanji's sated grin made Basho hard all over again. Kanji raised himself on one elbow, moving off Basho's sweaty body slightly. He glanced down, taking Basho's hand in his grip.

"You make me feel like this, too." He gazed down into Basho's face. "I have to go. I hadn't planned on this, but I have no regrets. I hope you don't either?"

"No, I don't." But Basho did. He had a horrible feeling he would be treated the same way Matilda was. Why oh why had he allowed this to happen?

"Would you like to spend the day together tomorrow?"

Basho, though surprised, nodded eagerly. "Yes, please."

Kanji laughed. "Good." He slipped off the bed.

"Would you like to take a shower?"

"No way." Kanji dressed quickly. "I want your scent all over my body."

Basho nodded, embarrassed but thrilled. Nobody had ever said such things to him. He got off the bed and followed Kanji out.

"Naked," the other man said, gathering Basho in his arms at the front door. They kissed. Their mutual heat was still there.

Kanji smiled again. So many times in one day. "See you tomorrow." He opened the front door, closed it behind him, and with that he was gone.

For a long moment Basho stood, their frantic lovemaking replaying in his mind. Wow. It had been intense. Intoxicating. He felt weird.

What do I do with myself now? He turned and walked to the bathroom, bracing himself for the moment he examined his bruised neck in the mirror.

Except he was unmarked. He checked all the places Kanji had bitten him, but apart from feeling tender, there was no sign of a mark or bruise. Relieved, he showered, but for some reason, the hot water bothered his skin. So did soap.

How weird.

He normally loved hot showers. He adored his bar soap. He switched to cold water and soaped up his hands, running them over his body. Every inch of him felt sore and very sensitive. He towel-dried gently and dressed, aware of the texture of each item of clothing he put on. Nothing felt right against his skin.

And then something else happened. He could see shadows and light he'd never experienced before. His eyes hurt when he glanced at the neon clock on the oven. He suddenly heard his next-door neighbor talking on his cell phone. Arguing with somebody about a sumo wrestling match. How bizarre. Basho had never even seen the man much less heard him talking through the walls.

Basho cleaned up the soup bowls, made a list of the things he still needed and left the apartment. Outside, his eyes hurt more, and his ears were sensitive to the slightest sound. He began seeing what looked like ghostly figures on the street.

It scared the crap out of him. He saw two little girls in old-fashioned garb walking down the street. The next second, they were gone.

A car honked him and he realized he'd stopped dead in the middle of the road.

He jumped back to the curb, his hands shaking. He wanted to go home, but he was afraid. What the hell was going on with him?

Basho retraced his steps, relieved when he got home, except that the pinging of the elevator door—so loud!—made him scream.

He stayed on his sofa, the TV annoying to all his senses. He slept on and off, feeling better as the day went on. Late in the evening, he felt wide awake and excited. There was a world out there. He had to explore it!

Basho went out again and shopped for all the things he needed. He'd do one more food shop before his family arrived, but he had plenty for now. He walked the streets, carrying his store bags. He gazed into windows, shocked when he saw the ghosts of the two little girls again. They held hands crossing a street. He tried to follow them, but they disappeared.

He stopped for a glass of wine at Olé, a Spanish wine bar and restaurant in the Lang Kwai Fong district. He'd always wanted to go there but had never felt comfortable going in alone. Now he seemed to be the life of the party, making jokes with the staff and drinking two glasses of sangria. He allowed the bartender to talk him into ordering chorizo and garlic shrimp tapas. Delicious.

As Basho walked home, purchases in hand, he decided this had been the best day of his life. Full of energy, he was surprised that he broke into a run, not even working up a sweat by the time he reached his building. Inside the apartment, he found homes for the chopstick set he'd just bought. Not to mention the six bottles of wine he'd picked up at Olé.

He had tried all afternoon not to think of Kanji but he couldn't help checking his cell phone repeatedly for calls or texts. The only person who had made contact was his mother, to let him know she, Hiroshi, and Liang were coming next Saturday, a week ahead of schedule.

Oh, joy.

Basho prowled his apartment, not sleepy, yet anxious to be in bed.

With Kanji.

All night he was up, cleaning, rearranging things, his thoughts never far from the man he was now sexually obsessed with.

He fell asleep as dawn broke, but was soon awakened by a knock at the door. He didn't even have to ask who it was. He knew it was Kanji.

He let the man in, overjoyed to see him. Kanji seemed pleased to greet him, too. They shut the door and began mauling each other, fucking with wild abandon on the floor. This time the biting felt as though Kanji was burning. It was the only part of their crazy sex that Basho didn't like.

Kanji kept him in bed most of the day, but Basho began to ache all over again. Just like the day before.

"I don't know what's happening to me," he said, frightened when the pain became excruciating.

"You're really hurting," Kanji said, and held him, soothing him with hugs and kisses until he fell asleep again.

When Kanji said he needed to leave at nightfall, Basho didn't mind. He was relieved to be alone and in pain. Did he have some twenty-four hour bug or something?

Near dawn, he felt better. He took a cold shower and made some steak and rice, thinking how weird that he'd suddenly become a night owl.

At work the next day, Kanji wasn't there, but Basho felt weird and shaky. He missed the other man's body. He missed his kisses and even the biting.

He'd been home about five minutes that evening when Kanji showed up.

Their frenetic, passionate lovemaking was the same. This time the biting was worse than ever. Basho sobbed at one point, but Kanji merely apologized and held him.

The next few days were so confusing to Basho, who was unable to focus on anything except the weird changes he was experiencing.

One night, after a vigorous bout of lovemaking, he dozed off and awoke to see a large tiger sitting on the bedroom floor looking at him. The tiger watched him with unblinking eyes. *My God.* They were Kanji's eyes.

"Kanji?" Basho called out, trembling with utter fear.

The tiger padded out, tail swishing.

Basho almost tripped over his own feet following the creature. He walked bang-slap into Kanji coming out of the bathroom.

"Relax," Kanji said, taking him in his arms. Basho allowed the other man to calm him. When Kanji gave him little nips along his neck and shoulders, Basho came.

"Wonderful," Kanji said against his lips. "Pain always turns to pleasure."

On Thursday, Basho thought about canceling his massage with Haku. He felt it would be cheating on Kanji if he got a hand job, but his body ached so much, he felt a massage was necessary. He would just decline the happy ending.

In Haku's little studio, with his masseur's gentle touch and soothing music to pamper him, Basho could almost believe he'd dreamed the weird stuff that had happened to him. He now craved the biting, but sensed some kind of frustration from Kanji, as though he wasn't reacting the right way.

"Your body is a mess," Haku said. "What have you been doing to yourself?"

"Nothing," Basho said.

"You're tense and your skin feels, I don't know . . . like you have bristles all over it."

Bristles? Basho sat up on the table. "What do you mean bristles?"

"Do you shave?" Haku asked, running his hands along Basho's chest and shoulders.

"No." He lay down again but his mind roiled. He declined the happy ending and a shower. Haku's bathroom overlooking the street was just too noisy.

That night, Kanji took him to dinner at a little restaurant with no name, tucked into a dark alleyway. Typical Hong Kong. The food was amazing, and the two men shared a gigantic porterhouse steak and broiled chicken.

They raced home to make love, but this time, Kanji bit him the second they fell on the bed. The pain that ripped through Basho's body was intense.

"What are you doing? What are you doing?" he screamed, jumped out of bed and grabbed his neck as a massive spurt of blood shot out of a vein. He became lightheaded both with the tremendous fear and the blood loss.

Kanji got out of bed and stared at him. "It's true. Damn." He gazed down at the floor.

"What's true?" Basho shouted. "I'm fucking dying here!" He raced for the phone, clamping the fingers of his right hand over the torn vein to stem the blood flow. He'd seen *Doc Martin* do this on TV to a man with a fearsome injury, and although the wound ached, Basho could no longer feel his life force dripping between his fingers.

He half-sobbed and half-yelled as he hobbled to the kitchen, blood dropping to his pristine floors.

I can't believe it. I really can't believe it.

To his shock, the landline phone had no dial tone.

"I'd read and heard that the Han Chinese were the only

ones who couldn't be turned."

"Turned?"

"I'm a werecat," Kanji said. "I thought . . . I thought if I tried hard enough, it would happen." He grabbed a kitchen towel and held it to Basho's throat. "I never meant to hurt you."

"What's a werecat?" But Basho already knew. He'd seen the tiger. He thought it was a ghastly dream. "I love you," he said. "But this was some kind of game for you?"

"Not a game. And love? What do you mean love? We have incredible sex, but I never said I was in love."

Basho thought he would fall apart right there and then.

Kanji led him to the bathroom, where he licked Basho's wounds, closing up the vein.

"I will never hurt you again," he said over and over.

No, you won't, because I am never allowing you near me again.

But Kanji stayed and even made love to him again, this time, tender and dear. Basho felt neither human nor animal. He felt attached to Kanji yet far away from him.

"My attempt to turn you has left you in some kind of limbo," Kanji confessed deep in the night. "I'm so sorry, Basho."

Basho was sorry, too.

He cleaned up his own blood in the morning, determined to be done with this . . . werecat.

And yet, he craved him. Even Kanji's merest touch soothed his anguished skin and soul. Early in the morning, somebody knocked at his front door.

Basho threw on pants and a shirt, ignoring Kanji's entreaties not to open it.

To Basho's dismay, he stood, with Kanji beside him, staring at his mother, brother, and new stepfather.

His mother smiled but Liang got a weird look on his face.

"That's not Basho!" he said, and started to scream.

Chapter Four

Basho was so riveted by his little brother's declaration that, for a second, he didn't immediately notice what was going on between Kanji and his mother. It was the way Liang turned his head and stared that caused Basho to grab Liang and pull him closer for safety.

Kanji was continuing to back up across the room, the look on his face one of mortal terror. The woman who had stood at his door no longer resembled his mother. Her eyes. There was something about her eyes and the sounds coming from her . . . my God, she was growling. Threatening growls of an angry wild animal filled the entire room . . . and her eyes were glowing amber.

The man at her side, the new husband didn't move a muscle. He seemed almost paralyzed.

Basho blinked. The window flew wide open and there was a flash of something. Kanji was gone.

"I knew it," she said. "I sensed it. It's why I'm here."

Basho shook his head. "I don't . . . what just . . ." The room was spinning. Darkness closed in and he was falling.

When Basho's eyes opened, he was lying on the sofa. His mother was sponging his forehead with a cool cloth. He felt as if he were in the Twilight Zone. This wasn't in her nature at all. "What are you doing?" he asked.

She smiled almost tenderly. Okay, where was his mother? Who was this woman?

Her husband and Liang hovered in the background, looking on anxiously.

"I feared this might happen." She put the cloth aside. "I wasn't at all sure he was here. I don't know how he found you. A very smart one, he is."

Basho struggled into a sitting position. "You're talking about Kanji."

"Is that what he calls himself?" She scoffed and moved away, pacing a little.

Basho got off the sofa, impatient. "Mother!"

"First," she said, "the stranger rice." She glanced at Hiroshi. "You must be polite. We eat."

Basho was in no mood for food but his mother was not going to budge. "I made some stranger rice. It's in the refrigerator," he said.

Mudan Loy stared at him. "Did you feed him with it?"

"You mean Kanji?" Basho suddenly felt guilty of something.

"Yes, him," she sneered. "Quick, an answer!"

"Ah . . . yes. Why? Tell me what's happening? I feel like death and I . . . I don't know. Sometimes the sounds are so loud . . . and I think he tried to—"

"Turn you," she interrupted. "He told you, didn't he?" She took out the rice and put it into a pan, and began to reheat it. "He told you what he was?"

Basho put his face in his hands. "It can't be true."

Mudan Loy glanced at Liang and Hiroshi. "Go and watch television." She looked at Basho. "You do have a working television in your bedroom?"

"Yes, of course." He stared as the man and boy walked into his room like trained robots. He turned to his mother. "You knew about Kanji, that he was some sort of animal?"

His mother turned down the temperature on the stove. "I shouldn't have kept this from you, Basho. I knew one day he'd find you. I thought that if I distanced myself from my children that it would be harder. He found you in New York, and he has just enough charm to seduce."

"Find me? Why would he be looking for me? Am I one of those . . . am I some sort of a cat?" He could hardly say it. "And what in hell are you, I mean . . . I saw your eyes and he was afraid of you."

"Watch your language," she scolded. "Speak to me with respect or not at all."

Basho sighed impatiently. "Forgive me." He bowed. "But you must understand that I'm beside myself. Am I dying?"

"No," she said. "But he is." Her eyes sparked gold when she said that.

Basho's heart fell. Yes, he was afraid and, yes, Kanji had hurt him with his bites. But, damn it, Basho had deep feelings already for him . . . whatever he was. "Why? Why is he dying?"

"He is the only survivor of his clan and his time is running out. Long ago, the Han, our people, were at war with his. His people were a clan of shapeshifters who preyed on the Han. Our flesh sustained the clan, due to the strength of our bloodline. Tired of being prey to the shape shifters, the Han began to fight back. It is how we became such fierce warriors, and the legend began that we could not be turned."

"So the Han wiped out the shifters?"

"Practically. They were desperate to find mates, and there was a scarcity among their own, so once again they attempted to turn the Han. It was virtually impossible by then, but they became more determined than ever. They wanted to take us into their bloodline."

He watched his mother lift the lid on the saucepan and stir the fragrant contents.

"And did they turn our ancestors?"

"They tried, but there was great resistance." She turned and looked at him. "Some of us carry the recessive gene. The traits come out from time to time, but we are not shifters.

Kanji's shifters were not able to turn us. They turned to other people but still their numbers dwindled as we continued to hunt them."

"But if they can't turn us, why did Kanji single me out? What does he want with me?"

"You're different."

Basho sank into the chair. "How?"

"Your father, he too carried the recessive gene. They captured him and tried to turn him. He died during the transformation."

"Then you lied to me!" Basho jumped to his feet.

"Yes, but to protect you. You are the product of two Hans with recessive shifter genes. Although it would be a challenge, Kanji believes that maybe you'd survive the transition. If he can turn you, you can then turn anyone with Han blood in their veins. He would revive the clan, and continue to survive."

Basho wanted to laugh. He wanted to cry. This sounded incredible but looking back to the first time they'd met, the way Kanji had looked at him, the way he'd insisted on Basho taking the job. It was true. It was all true.

"What do we do?" Basho asked as his mother spooned stranger rice into four bowls.

"We eat," she said.

Basho wanted to protest, but she fixed him with her stare, which meant there was no use arguing with her. "Go and get your brother and stepfather, please?"

"Do they know all this?" Basho asked her.

"Hiroshi has worked on the African safari, hunting rogue animals. It's why I married him."

Fear crawled up and down Basho's spine. "You're going to send him after Kanji!"

"Please get them so we can eat. The food is growing cold."

A few minutes later they were all sitting around the table.

Basho couldn't eat. This was too much, and still he didn't understand. His mother had known all along and she'd lied about everything, shipping her children off and away from her, to protect them from Kanji.

As they ate, Basho couldn't help wondering if any of his other siblings had this so-called gene.

"No," his mother said out of the blue. "Only you."

He blinked. "What? Did you just . . . oh my God! Have you always been able to read my mind?"

She nodded, her mouth full. "Yes."

"How embarrassing," he muttered.

Liang laughed. "Especially when you thought about sex, eh, brother?"

Basho gave his little brother a dirty look. "Never mind."

"The stranger rice is good. The best I've ever eaten," Hiroshi announced.

The sound of his voice boomed across the table.

"It was the first time Basho had heard him speak. He nodded at him. "Thank you."

Then in his head, he could have sworn he heard the man say, "Lamb isn't bad. Have you ever tried cooking it with human meat?"

Basho gasped, staring at him.

The man just smiled, then returned to eating his meal.

Basho took some time to study him now—beefy, broad shoulders, heavy features, and his arms were roped with muscles. *A hunter. He's a hunter.* There was something wrong, something very wrong here. He didn't know what, but he had to find out.

The meal seemed to go on endlessly. He couldn't be rude and just jump up from the table, but he needed to find Kanji. He needed to hear what he had to say?

You will do no such thing.

He looked over to see his mother's gaze on him. They were

talking about a boutique she wanted to take a look at, but still he could hear her voice in his head.

You have been seduced by him. He will try and try but he won't be able to turn you. He will abandon you to die. He will kill us all if we let him. He must be hunted down.

AND SHOT!

Basho's head turned to see Liang looking at him. Oh no, he, too, was part of this hunting party. Basho quickly looked away. He told himself not to think about anything except that bowl in front of him. He tried to eat. He swallowed a mouthful and felt sick. He scraped back the chair. "Excuse me."

He took a run for the bathroom. He heaved but nothing came up, so he leaned against the wall in a cold sweat. I don't believe Kanji wanted to hurt me. He healed me. He licked the bite wound I had. He is not bad. I won't let them kill him.

Somehow, he had to get out of here. Outside the bathroom, he could hear them talking, planning their next move. He felt in his pocket for his cellphone. He couldn't call but he could text him. He took a breath. What if he was doing the wrong thing? What if Kanji really want to kill them all? He'd told him already that it was just sex. But it didn't matter. He couldn't just stand by and watch them hunt down Kanji. Basho needed to hear his side of the story even if it killed him.

Basho brought up Kanji's number and typed: Kanji, I must see you. Are you there? Please answer me.

He waited.

"Basho!" His mother pounded on the door. "Are you all right?"

"Fine." He looked at his phone. *Come on, come on, come on.*

Then: Are you alone?

No. They are all around me. I must see you. You must tell me the truth. They will hunt you.

How do I know it's not a trap?

You don't. I don't know if you will kill me or not either. So, we both take a risk???

Wait until tomorrow. Leave for work like normal but come to the Mandarin Hotel. Text me from the lobby and make sure you're not followed.

And you'll tell me everything?

He waited. There was no answer.

Basho deleted the entire conversation, then left the bathroom.

"You look pale," his mother said. "Are you feeling better?"

He nodded. "Look, I don't want to be a bad host but do you mind if I show you all where to sleep and I go to bed? I'm very tired and it's late. I need to go to work tomorrow."

"You are not going to work for him!" My mother raised a hand to her heart as if she would fall over.

Basho shook his head. "I'm going in to give my resignation of course. And Kanji won't be there."

"That we know. He is a snake hiding in the grass," Hiroshi boomed. "He will feel the sting soon."

Basho winced inwardly. "Yes, I guess, and he isn't usually there during the day all the time. He's busy."

Liang came over and placed a hand on Basho's shoulder. "It's easy to get attached, brother."

When in hell did he get so knowledgeable about these things?

"Mother filled me in," he said.

"You, too . . . you read my thoughts." I thought I saw the glow of gold in his eyes for a moment. I backed up.

"Basho." He put out his hands. "It comes out in me, too, sometimes, but I'm not a pure breed like you. I'm only—"

"Liang!" Mudan Loy snapped. "Enough. Go to bed, son."

Liang's head fell.

"I'll ah . . . show you where to sleep," Basho said, taking his brother's elbow. The boy clearly knew more than he was letting on.

In the den, Basho closed the door. "For privacy," he said when Liang gave him a curious look. "There are sheets and a pillow on the chair," he pointed. "I'll get you a blanket."

"I won't need it. I'm usually very warm."

"Liang?" Basho came closer. "What are you not telling me?"

He looked at the sheets. "Nice color."

"Look at me." Basho took his chin between his fingers.

"I can't," he said.

"She's lying to me. Why?"

Liang shook his head.

"Have you changed? Can you?"

"No!" He looked horrified. He scrambled to get away from him, then fell over the chair.

The noise caused Mudan Loy and her new husband to push into the room.

Basho was helping his brother to his feet.

"I tripped," Liang muttered. "I'm good."

Mudan Loy and Hiroshi stood looking at Basho for a few minutes. Basho thought only of how he would hand in his resignation the next day. Satisfied, the two left the room.

The conversation, if there was to be one, was over. His brother was scared of something or someone. Basho dared not think too much about who it might be.

When he came into the kitchen again, his mother was finishing the washing up. "I would have helped you," he said.

"I don't mind." She smiled at him but it didn't quite reach her eyes.

"I'm giving you my room," he told her. "You will be comfortable in there. I just need to get Liang a blanket."

"I'll take it to him," Hiroshi offered.

Basho nodded. "I'll get it."

His mother followed him into the room. Basho jumped when she touched his shoulder.

"Know this," she said, taking the blanket, "I've always done my best for you."

"Of course," he said.

"This is a nice room."

"Thank you."

It smells like animals were fucking in here. Blood . . . semen . . . cat.

Basho caught his breath and looked at her. "What?"

"Nothing dear." She smiled. "I'll just go and say goodnight to Liang now."

Alone in the room, he glanced at the bed and realized that the bed was made up with fresh sheets. But he knew that he hadn't had the time to make up the room before they'd arrived. Had his mother done it when he'd had his blackout? If so, then she knew he and Kanji had been intimate. It seemed she knew everything.

Slowly, he made his way back to the kitchen. His mother was sipping tea. "Where is Hiroshi?" he asked.

"He went for a walk," she said.

"Is he one, too?"

She put down her teacup. "One what?"

"Is he a shifter?"

"Of course not." She laughed. "He's a hunter."

"And what are you and Liang?"

She stood. "We are your family," she grunted. "Now, I will retire. Goodnight, son." She walked into the bedroom and shut the door.

Basho walked over to the window and looked out. He took out the phone.

Where are you? My mother has a hunter with her. He's out. Maybe he's looking for you.

There was no reply.

Kanji, are you all right? The man my mother married is a hunter. He is trying to kill you.

I know.

You know?

Yes.

Are you safe?

I am. Go to sleep, Basho.

I can't.

Stop worrying about me.

You know why.

Yes.

It doesn't matter that you don't care.

I never said I didn't care. Good night.

Basho erased the conversation and closed his phone. He stayed by the window and waited. Then a scent filled his nose. He breathed in some air, then saw his new stepfather walk around the corner. Damn. He could smell him and yet, he wasn't a shifter. Was he? No. Kanji had bit him but nothing had happened. He'd simply bled. Would another bite have turned him or killed him?

The door opened. "Hello, Basho. Waiting for me?"

A flash of gold and then it was gone. Basho shut down his thoughts because now he knew that Hiroshi could also read his mind.

"Ah, Mother has gone to bed," Basho said. "You can go anytime."

Hiroshi sat down in the chair by the door. "I'm kind of a night owl. Not tired yet." Hiroshi was studying Basho carefully. "You do realize that your boss is a killer."

Basho nodded.

"When he has changed, he doesn't care who or what he kills. It is the blood he craves. He must be put down."

"I haven't read of any animal attacks," Basho offered.

"He covers his kill. He's a human, too, so he's clever."

Basho swallowed. He couldn't believe that Kanji would just indiscriminately kill people.

"Why? Is it because you've fallen in love with him?" Hiroshi demanded.

Basho shook his head. "Of course not."

"Your mother changed your cum-stained sheets while you were blacked out."

Basho felt himself blush crimson. "It was . . . a one-time thing."

"More than that. He made more than one attempt to turn you. I assume it is less painful during sex. There is a . . ." He lifted a hand. "Distraction."

Basho looked away.

"I'm not judging you. I've seen enough of that sort of thing in the animal world to know its natural enough. Just find yourself a human to fuck, Basho." He stood. "Well, I think I will turn in. Sweet dreams."

Basho sat on the sofa. He leaned back and closed his eyes. This was a nightmare, but even more than he'd imagined. He had made up so many stories about a girlfriend and his fantastic life. He'd been so worried about any type of confrontation with his mother. He'd assumed when the moment arrived that it was going to be about his sexuality, but that seemed to have taken a backseat to something a hell of a lot more explosive. "Kanji," he whispered in the dark. "I need you."

CHAPTER FIVE

Basho left the house at dawn before anyone was awake and headed for Connaught Road. He didn't take a shower, shave, or change his clothes. He went directly to the legendary Mandarin Hotel.

In the lobby, he sent Kanji a text. He looked around nervously as he waited for an answer. It seemed that all eyes were on him. *Kanji, I'm here. Please. Don't make me wait too long.*

Nothing.

Twice, hotel security came over to speak to him. He looked kind of unkempt and he was just loitering, which was strictly forbidden. "I'm waiting for someone," he said in Chinese. "I have a meeting."

Finally, a text popped up. Maybe he'd willed it from looking at his phone so hard.

Take the elevator to the tenth floor. I'll meet you.

Basho walked across the lobby. Luckily no one stopped him. He pressed the elevator and waited. A man stepped off a minute later and he got on and pressed 10.

On the tenth floor, the elevator door slid open. He stepped out onto the carpeted hallway and waited. "Come on," he sighed, looking around.

He had another text. *Room 1010.*

Basho hurried along the hallway and turned the corner. Room 1010 was right at the end. He braced himself, had stored up all the questions he needed to ask. The door opened before he could knock. Kanji stood there, fresh from a shower, towel wrapped around his perfect body, and Basho was without words.

Kanji reached out, pulled him into the room and closed the door. He walked over to the sofa. It was a suite, large and luxurious, with a view of the city through two walls of glass. The suite was filled with elegant furnishings and stylishly decorated with timber paneling fashioned from Chinese elm. He spotted some beautiful jade statues beside a king-sized bed. "Wow."

"Take a look around," Kanji said. "I'm getting dressed."

Oh really. Don't.

Kanji glanced at him.

Basho had forgotten that Kanji could read his thoughts. "Damn," he said softly. "I'm going to check out the bathroom." He was happy to disappear.

The bathroom was beside the spacious bedroom and something to see. There were two marble basins, a walk-in shower, and a breathtaking stand-alone oval bathtub. The room looked bigger than his entire department. Basho sat on the edge of the tub for a minute.

When Kanji walked in, doing up his shirt, Basho stood. "Sorry, I was thinking."

"Don't blame you. There is a lot to think about."

"Kanji, what's happening?"

"I was honest with you, Basho. I told you what I was."

"You didn't tell me what I was." Basho met his gaze.

"I wasn't sure until I noticed that you weren't undergoing the transformation. Usually it only takes once and I can see it. But not with you."

"Why? Why would you pick me and why am I different?"

"Your ancestry is pure. You're one hundred percent Han."

"Which means what?" Basho asked, his voice sounding a little desperate.

Kanji sat on the bed. "Which means that if it would have worked, if I could have forced the shift in you, it would have reversed the curse. I was wrong to have done that. I shouldn't have taken you like that. I should have asked you, explained."

"Curse?"

He nodded. "A curse put on me centuries ago. It happened as I underwent a shamanistic initiatory crisis."

"A what?"

"It's a rite of passage for shamans-to-be, commonly involving physical illness and sometimes even psychological crisis."

"The Chuonnasuan," Basho said. "The last master shaman among the Tangus Peoples in the Northeast of China."

The wounded healer was an archetype for a shamanic journey. This process was important to the young shaman. She or he underwent a type of sickness that pushed her or him to the brink of death. "So you almost died?"

Kanji nodded. "Yes, but in the process, something happened. One of your ancestors put a curse on me. I crossed to the underworld, seeking vital information on how to heal myself and others who are sick."

"When the intended healer cures his own sickness, he or she has the knowledge to cure others," Basho added.

Kanji smiled. "You know of the ritual then?"

"Yes, but you said you were cursed?"

"By a ghost in the afterlife, a Han. It was a case of unrequited love. When I rejected her, the ghost was bitter and cursed me."

Basho was aghast. "A ghost cursed you?"

Kanji nodded. "I met the ghost of a beautiful female tiger on my death journey. She began as my spirit guide. She tried to keep me there with her but I couldn't stay. She turned me into a were-tiger. I could hardly believe it at first. You might laugh at this"—Kanji stared at him intently for a moment as though trying to assess Basho's reaction—"But I was a vegetarian before I was turned."

Basho didn't think it was funny. He thought the whole

thing tragic. Poor Kanji all alone, with a taste for blood he didn't like in the first place.

Kanji grew silent then said, "It was then she cursed me and, during the transformation from life to death, I shifted for the first time."

He lapsed into such lengthy silence that Basho gently prodded him. "What happened then?"

"I hunted and was hunted. At first I didn't realize that there were others like me. Other shifters. Lost, alone, scared. Feral. We were wild things who did not want to be that way."

"Among your people."

"No." Kanji looked at him. "Among yours."

Basho sucked in some breath. "Mudan Loy says you need to turn a pure blood to sustain your existence, that's why you tried to turn me. She says you are the last of your kind."

He shook his head. "Your mother is pure, and she has the power to shift."

"What? She told me my family didn't have that power." He thought for a moment. Man, his mother was such an accomplished liar. *That's where I acquired that skill set.*

He felt the weight of Kanji's scrutiny. "Then . . . do I? have that power" Basho looked at him.

Kanji nodded. "You will have it, but not without her first showing you how and when to initiate the first transformation."

Basho shuddered. "I don't trust her. Why does it have to be her?"

"Don't be afraid," Kanji said. "It must be a cooperative effort. She must show you and you must be willing."

"There's one thing I don't understand. You knew I was Han. You wanted me for that reason. You tried to bring on this transformation yet you knew you couldn't. Why did you keep biting me? You couldn't turn me. You are cursed and yet me getting that curse from you is impossible."

"It's not impossible." Kanji met Basho's gaze. "There are . . . certain conditions that can make it happen."

"What conditions? You just said only my mother can do it because we are Han."

"I can do it, but only under one provision. You must love me. And after that, submit. Once you submit and I take your blood, you will die."

Basho closed his eyes. When he opened them again, Kanji was looking out the window. "You could have done it. I confessed my love for you. Why didn't you just proceed, take what you came for?" Basho was on his feet, his voice loud. "Now, you don't have it and you're going to be hunted. You don't care about me and yet . . ."

"I never said that," Kanji turned to look at him, cutting off his words. "I never said I didn't care. Don't you see why I couldn't have you talk of love? To talk of love would have made it easy for you to give up your life. The one who cursed me made it so. It's ironic."

"So now," Basho said softly, "what do I do? Do I stand by and let you die?"

Kanji came closer and looked down into Basho's face. "No. Go, get as far away as you can from everyone and everything."

Basho reached up and touched his cheek. "I can't. I can't go. Kiss me."

"You should be afraid," he said, but he moved closer.

"No. I confessed my love. You could have taken advantage of that, forced the shift and taken your cure. You didn't. You healed me after you made me bleed. You care for me."

"No." Kanji pulling Basho into his arms. "I don't just care about you. I love you."

Basho surrendered to Kanji's kisses as he smothered Basho's mouth with his. Hands pulled at his shirt as Kanji's rough tongue lapped over each of Basho's taut nipples. Basho leaned back just a little to give Kanji access. His mouth on Basho's chest was making him crazy. He watched as the tongue extended and tasted each inch of skin, circling and then licking again, leaving each one wetter and stiffer with each stroke. One hand reached up and plucked at one of Basho's nipples, while his tongue again worked its magic on the other.

"Um, yes!" Basho cried out. The mouth clamped down on one while fingers flicked carelessly over the other, pulling and pinching. He felt a sharp pain as teeth grabbed his nipple like a claw then again suckled it gently. The pleasure was intense, like he could orgasm right there just from what he was doing with his mouth.

Basho's cock was so hard. "Um, Kanji, my cock."

Kanji looked at him and smiled. Basho saw the circle of gold, bright in his eyes. "I'll get to your cock." His hands went to Basho's waist. He undid his zipper with one hand and continued fondling him with the other. He pulled down his pants and pushed the briefs down with them. Basho's cock sprang forward, aching, needy. "I want to play with it," Kanji growled, pulling him forward and hotly kissing his mouth. Then he released it. "Go lie on the bed."

Basho eagerly fell onto the bed. He spread his thighs in anticipation, his fingers touching his torso. He was trying to recreate that sensation, the one he'd been getting from Kanji's furious licks. No such luck.

Kanji crawled on the bed on all fours straddling Basho's hips. Then just for a second, Basho saw it, the tiger, fierce, proud, and beautiful. The face of the man and the tiger interchanged for a moment, then stabilized back to Kanji.

Kanji lifted Basho's cock in his hand and played with it. He kind of batted at it at one point, like a cat would play with a mouse. Basho bit down on his bottom lip and drew blood. Kanji lifted his head and pressed his mouth to his, licking

Basho's lips.

Again, Kanji handled his cock, nuzzled his neck. Basho was on fire. He wrapped his legs around Kanji and squeezed tight. He seemed to rear back as if he needed to collect himself. Then he looked at him.

Basho saw the predatory look of an animal on the prowl, one that had its prey in its grasp and was about to ravish it.

He was inside Basho with one push. Basho felt him deep in his very soul. He was his. Kanji knew it because he seemed to relax before moving ever so slowly inside Basho's body. The pace sped up a little. Basho stroked Kanji's face as he looked down at him. "It's alright," Basho said. "I love you, Kanji. I know you love me, too. Take what you need. I'm yours."

Kanji's jaw opened. Basho saw the tiger's eyes, felt the soft fur against his skin. Then the shot rang out.

Kanji fell on top of Basho and went limp.

Basho screamed. "No, no. Kanji!"

Kanji was lifted off him. Basho looked up to see Hiroshi, Liang and Mudan Loy.

"Looks like we got here just in time," his mother said. "Cover yourself." She threw the blanket at him and clicked her tongue.

He watched with horror as Liang and Hiroshi started to carry Kanji's limp body out of the room. Basho tried to get up but his mother shoved him back. "You will stay put."

Tears stung Basho's eyes. "You had me followed."

"Of course. I knew you'd run after him, try to warn him. It's the reason he was cursed in the first place. He made some poor helpless girl fall for him, then left her flat."

The bitterness in her voice couldn't be mistaken.

"It was a ghost," Basho protested. "Some ghost when he was between life and death. He's a healer. And you've killed him."

"We haven't killed him. We have plans for him." She

smiled.

"Mother, I love him." Basho was ready to plead. "He loves me, too."

"Hah!"

"What do you have against Kanji? You don't even know him."

"He killed many of your people. Don't you care?"

"He was cursed. He couldn't control it."

"And he still can't."

"But this is personal," Basho accused. "Why is it personal?"

She didn't answer.

"He has lived a long time. He's immortal maybe. And us, are we immortal, mother?"

She shook her head.

Basho got off the bed and wrapped the sheet around him. "It's not because of the past. It's because in that curse lies his ability to heal, to heal himself and others. He can give you immortality."

"You were willing to die for him." She shook her head. "Do you know how precious life is?"

"I think so. Until I met Kanji I really had no clue. He made me bleed, but he healed me. He could have let me die, but saved me."

His mother seemed surprised. Then, she shook her head. "No. He is selfish. He had his reasons." She lifted a hand at Basho's protests. "Interesting to know though that he can heal more than just himself."

She shook her head. "He knows so little of his powers." She looked at him, her eyes filled with blood. "I'm dying."

He blinked and shook his head. "No."

"I've been given only six months. A rare form of cancer. I've known for some time. The doctors are amazed I've lasted this long. It's the Han blood. But I feel myself going."

"Can I heal you if you teach me to shift?"

"No. And I can no longer shift. I don't have the strength. It's takes stamina. Once the shift is made, there is no turning back. It's best that you don't ever try to do it."

"Why?"

She looked so sad, it stunned him. He could see years of infinite pain in her eyes. "We are forced to live in secrecy. To hunt the innocent. Sometimes, the not so innocent. We learn not to trust. We are not the same as everybody else."

"But you married a hunter."

"That's called keeping my enemies close. We have many of those, we shifters. They are legion."

She was tired and she was bitter, but he felt certain that now he knew his family's secret, they could finally be close. "Kanji can heal you."

She nodded. "Yes."

"Then why not tell him, ask him to heal you? Why shoot him?"

"Because I need to have retribution for my ancestors, Basho. I promised if I found him, I'd kill him. But now that I'm dying . . . and I know he has that healing power . . . he's a healer and because he's a shifter, he can cleanse me of the disease. But he must die after." She met Basho's gaze. "Who would you choose, him or your mother?"

"Don't ask me that." Basho sighed. "Where is he?"

"He is being taken to a safe place. He was shot with a tranquilizer. He will wake up soon."

"Does he have to bite you?"

"No," she said. "It's in the blood."

"How much blood do you need?"

She looked at him and smiled. Basho saw sharp teeth emerge. "A lot."

Chapter Six

The cage that Kanji was held in was housed in a deep basement. When Basho entered the basement with Mudan Loy, Hiroshi immediately protested. "Why did you bring him here? He's the enemy."

"He's not the enemy, he's my son," Mudan Loy said, finding a chair to sit down on.

Basho could see that she was tired. Why hadn't he noticed how pale and thin she was before?

"I've told him everything," she added, reaching for Basho's hand.

Basho's squeezed it. Then he heard a loud growling sound coming from the corner. Basho let go of his mother's hand and walked over to where Liang stood.

"See what we got," he said with a smirk.

Basho came closer to the iron cage. There on the floor of the cage lay a beautiful Bengal tiger trying to lift its head. Some metal contraption was attached to his side and Basho could see the blood flowing out.

"It's still drowsy." Liang laughed.

"*He's* still drowsy," Basho snapped, pushing him away. "What are you doing to him?" Basho pressed his face into the bars, his heart breaking. "I'm so sorry, Kanji." Basho turned around. "This isn't right. Let him go."

"You'll let your mother die then?"

"If it's her turn to die . . . then . . ." He broke off. "I'm sorry, Mother. I can't let you do this." He felt it. He felt it coming. With or without her, he was going to do this. He turned to the cage and met Kanji's sad, pain-filled eyes. "Help me. Help me do this. I know you can."

Hands grabbed at him and he turned, growling like an animal. Something was happening because Liang and Hiroshi backed up, their faces stricken with fear.

His mother stayed sitting, as if she had no strength to protest anymore. She watched.

Basho turned, broke the lock with one hand and pulled open the door. He leaned down and stroked the tiger's coat. Then he gently pulled out the needle. The blood gushed like a fountain and Basho leaned down and licked over the wound. When the wound instantly healed, he reared back, amazed.

He stood, his gaze picking up every little movement. Hiroshi took a threatening step forward. Liang stood beside Mudan Loy. Basho came out of the cage. "I'm sorry."

He heard a voice behind him, Kanji's voice. "Bring her to me," he said.

Basho turned to see Kanji in human form, struggle into a sitting position. Basho took off his shirt and placed it over Kanji's lap. Kanji smiled at him. "Bring her, Basho."

Basho looked at Mudan Loy. Liang drew her forward. "He won't hurt her."

Basho shook his head and took his mother's hand. He led her to the cage.

With all his strength, Kanji managed to rise to his feet. The shirt dropped to his feet but he didn't seem to notice. "Come closer," he whispered.

"Why?" Mudan Loy cried, tears running in rivers down her face. "Why would you do it?"

"I owe you," he whispered. "I owe your people." Then he said something that only Mudan Loy understood, some ancient language that left the others in the room in the dark.

She lowered her head.

Kanji's jaw opened and sharp tiger teeth appeared. When he lowered his jaw, Hiroshi stepped forward but Basho put up his hand. Kanji wasn't going to bite Mudan Loy. He was going to bite himself.

Basho cringed as Kanji opened a vein in his lower arm. He lifted it to Mudan Loy's mouth. "Drink," he said softly.

Sobbing, blood smeared across her lips, she opened her mouth and took the elixir he offered. She drank deeply until Kanji began to sway on his feet. He pulled away and Mudan Loy collapsed in Basho's arms.

"He's killed her," Liang accused.

"No," Kanji grunted, sliding back to the floor. "She is healing. She must take the journey as I did. She will come back. She will live." Kanji's eyes closed.

Hiroshi and Liang carried Mudan Loy out of the cage, and Basho dropped to his knees beside Kanji. He pulled him close and held him. "Please, Kanji, don't die on me. Don't die."

Basho wasn't sure how much time went by before he heard a voice say something.

"I'm sorry, Basho," Hiroshi said suddenly behind him. "He's lost a lot of blood. I'm not sure he'll survive."

Basho's face was wet with tears as he kissed Kanji's soft hair. He couldn't speak. Every second he heard Kanji's heart beating was a blessing even if he was unconscious.

"Your mother is conscious. Basho, I think it worked. I think the cancer is gone."

He nodded and squeezed Kanji tight. His mother would live and the man he loved would die. He rocked him a little, whispering in his ear. "I will always love you."

"Basho."

He turned to see his mother standing there. Yes, something had changed. She looked fit, well. She walked into the cage and stroked Basho's head. "There is one possibility."

Basho looked up at her. "Anything."

"Your blood. You, a pure Han, can give him a blood transfusion. I'm not sure what effect it will have on him. It might reverse the curse, let him live as a human. He will no longer be what he is, but he will live. Perhaps."

"And what is the worst case?" Basho looked up at her.

"Your blood will kill him."

"He never said that. He never said if I gave him my blood, it might kill him."

"He was willing to risk it. He wanted to reverse the curse that badly. Hiroshi can set it up." Mudan Loy glanced at her husband and nodded.

Hiroshi hooked up the tube to both Basho and Kanji, making sure that Basho's blood was going into Kanji's vein. Basho watched his face anxiously for any sign as the blood transfused. "If I see anything that looks like it's having a negative effect on him," Basho told Hiroshi, "you will take it out."

Hiroshi stood by. Even his mother and brother watched as the minutes ticked by. Nothing. There was no indication that the blood transfusion had helped or hurt Kanji. Hiroshi removed the tubes and took them away.

"Come on," Mudan Loy said. "You need to eat."

"No," Basho said. "I need to be with my love."

His mother sighed.

"I don't care what you think," Basho said. "I love him. He loves me. And I will stay with him until the end, no matter what. Now, leave us."

Hiroshi put his arm around his wife and they left. Liang lingered a moment. "I'm sorry," he said softly. "Really." Then he, too, was gone.

Basho nodded, tears in his eyes. He hugged Kanji to him. "You saved my mother. You gave your life."

Basho's eyes closed. The loss of blood had taken its toll. He was tired. He had no idea how long he'd slept.

When he opened his eyes, he was alone. "Kanji?" He

shouted. He stumbled to his feet. "Kanji!"

"Here."

Basho's head turned to see Kanji standing a few feet away. He struggled to his feet and ran to him. Wrapping his arms around him, he held on tight. "Are you all right?"

He nodded, kissing Basho's forehead. "You saved my life."

Basho smiled. "You are now my slave."

Kanji laughed. "Don't be so sure."

"Are you . . . did it take away the curse?"

Kanji shook his head. "No, but I feel more in control than I have ever been."

"Really? I always thought you were very much in control."

"Ah. So my macho act worked, huh? It always worked until I met you. And now I have a craving for stranger rice. And you. I can't decide which I want first. What have you done to me, Basho?"

Basho grinned. "I want to shift. I want to know what you feel."

Kanji hugged him. "One day, when you're ready."

"Then it was a myth that my blood could reverse your curse?"

"Seems like."

"I'm so sorry."

"I'm not sorry at all." He smiled.

Basho wrinkled his nose. "I don't understand."

"If I hadn't believed the myth, I wouldn't have pursued you like I did. I'd lost all faith I'd ever find love. But you are love, Basho. And it doesn't matter what else I am because you love me in spite of it."

"Oh, baby," he said, hugging Kanji to him. "I will always love you, in whatever shape or form you are."

"And I, you," he said.

Basho suddenly heard the scurrying of a mouse in the basement. He turned his head and caught sight of the mouse just as it was about to scurry into a hole. If he'd reached out he could have picked it up by the tail. In his mind, he pictured one big paw clamping down on it and tossing it up in the air.

When he glanced back at Kanji, Kanji was smiling at him. "Guess we'll have to get you out of this basement and find something to eat unless of course you wish to stay down here and decrease the mouse population?"

Basho smiled a secret smile. "Naw, I don't want to work that hard for my supper just yet."

"Will you make me some stranger rice again, with pork?"

"Sure. But maybe not tonight, sweet man. Let's order out. I need to save my strength." He kissed Kanji's mouth. "For later."

Kanji nodded enthusiastically. "Sounds like a good plan." He threw an arm around Basho and they headed up the basement stairs and out into the sunlight.

You may also enjoy the following from eXtasy Books Inc:

Ghost Flower
A.J. Llewellyn and D.J. Manly

Excerpt

Feng returned to the dream, seeing drops of blood falling from the bubbles his cousin had blown and he had destroyed. The blood fell on his cheeks and down to his feet.

Feet. He suddenly became aware of dancing feet. A row of women in beautiful, long, pale green dresses with over-sized sleeves began dancing and singing in front of him. Their moves were so graceful but so often extended it looked as if they might be marionettes on the verge of falling. The music was whimsical, their steps entrancing when he caught glimpses of them under the sweep of their gowns.

His gaze flew up into the face of a beautiful young woman. He knew her. And she knew him. With each swirl of her long sleeves, she aged before his eyes.

Mrs. Wei!

Who was Mrs. Wei? He searched his memory. It was just there. Just out of reach. He knew she was dead. He knew he missed her. He begged her not to leave him. For the second time in three nights, his heart, his feelings of love, were coming back to him. He knew he missed Mrs. Wei dreadfully.

And then he remembered—he'd found her dead body. In life, she'd been a famous ta ge dancer as a young woman. Then she'd aged. Her movements as he watched were graceful and gorgeous. She was no longer in pain. She charmed and touched him. But how did he know her?

The woman and all those around her formed a pattern like petals, their skirts billowing with slashes of crimson as they danced in small, tight circles. They sang like angels.

Angels!

Remember!

Mrs. Wei stepped forward. "You must return to him. You must remember. You must go back. His sacrifice is too great. You must return when the ghost flower blossoms."

"No!" he yelled as one by one the women popped and disappeared, small rainbows on his soul. He heard their voices still singing in perfect harmony. Tears ran down his cheeks. Don't leave me. Tell me what to remember! He longed to shout this out, but the words stuck like dry rice in his throat.

He awoke suddenly, realizing this song was on the radio. Disappointment shook his bones. She had been real. She had loved him. He was certain of that. And what the heck was a ghost flower?

Warm hands moved over his belly and chest. Russell. He'd been so closed to the man for weeks now. He tried not to stiffen as Russell kissed the back of Feng's neck, nuzzling him. He tried to relax. He loved Russell, really he did, but it had morphed into a different kind of love.

Halloween was only days away. He wondered what had happened to Ki, the man he'd had a crush on until he met . . . met . . . whom had he met? He drew a blank.

Russell was hard and obviously excited because he was humping Feng's ass cheeks now, his glistening cockhead beating an insistent tattoo against Feng's crack. Feng didn't want to sigh and bit down on the urge, in spite of his feelings of restlessness. He was surprised how wet Russell was, his cock leaking before they'd even started.

Giving the guy head was less intrusive than taking him up the ass. In the past, Feng had loved getting fucked. The sounds and smells of early morning sex inflamed his soul, giving heat to his dormant fantasies.

That's what it was! How could he have forgotten? His mind had dried up since his return. It was a desert of the soul. No dreams, no idyll. He could give Russell what he wanted in exchange for information. Feng turned around swiftly, one eye on the time. Six-forty in the morning. The red lanterns of LA's Chinatown which swung high outside their windows were still alight, giving Feng a sense of comfort. There was something about them he knew he should remember.

He just didn't know what.

Sex would be over in fifteen minutes. Russell always took very cold showers with salt-soap and birch branches for exactly three minutes each morning. Then he walked over the cobblestone path to the old Chinatown Square to the comic bookstore he'd taken over almost as soon as they'd returned from their strange sojourn a year ago.

In decades past, it had been a ginseng store and the smell still permeated the old quarter. Sometimes, Russell pretended their journey to the other side never happened. Sometimes, he remembered a lot more than he cared to admit. Feng knew this because Russell, who'd longed to be a manga artist, had caved in to the god of money and worked a 'necessary' job instead of following his passion.

Once he came back, he pursued his art, literally. He'd started producing graphic novels that were, frankly, very weird. In them, Russell seemed to pine for a place, some . . . sanctuary. Hey, maybe they weren't so different after all. Russell's comics were about Russell, a boy, who lived in a fantasy world.

He once told Feng that his inspiration had been Feng himself. But Feng couldn't remember being in a fantasy world. Ever. And he remembered nothing of his life before he died.

Died? What made him think that? The idea didn't panic him . . . it just seemed . . . unreal. And of course, it was. Except that lately Russel's comic books reflected more and more glimmers of what had happened to them in their adventures on what Feng had begun to think of as the other side.

He moved around so his mouth captured Russell's cock in one, long, fluid motion. Gazing up to watch his lover through his half-closed eyes, Feng saw the look of surprise on Russell's face. Feng had been so disinterested for weeks and now, he knew, Russell was ecstatic.

"Oh, baby," he said, threading his hands through Feng's hair. Feng sucked Russell, giving it all he had. He had questions to ask and he was convinced Russell had the answers. A little sugar from Feng and it felt certain Russell would give him the answers he needed.

He ticked them off in his mind. Who is the man who haunts my dreams? Why can't I see his face but why do I feel . . . no, I know he loves me? What is a ghost flower? Who is Mrs. Wei? Why am I excited that Halloween is coming? Does it have something to do with . . . him?

Feng felt Russell's excitement and kept his throat open, his lips tight, giving the man a mind-blowing thrill. Russell always tasted good. His lover fell back against the bed, his mouth softer in repose. He'd been so tense with Feng lately. Amazing what a bit of sex could do to a man.

"Shower with me," Russell said, but Feng balked. He saw no pleasure or real medicinal value in using the salt-soap and flogging himself with tree branches, but Russell swore by these things. Feng lingered in bed, wanting to clean his teeth and rinse his mouth as soon as Russell walked out the door. Russell came back, naked, and wet, looking cheerful, his skin blush-pink from the workout he'd given it with the birch branches. He looked healthy and glowing, his smile cheerful. Maybe Feng should consider beating himself up a little. Maybe it would perk him up. Russell was always so damned chipper these days, except for the area of their sex life.

Russell toweled off quickly, dressing in his usual jeans and long-sleeved gray Gap sweater. Russell wore a lot of gray lately. His comic books were gray, too. He did not write the series, called Shades of Gray under his own name. He just used initials. R.B. His illustrations were dark, his stories also dark. His character, Russell, was on a metaphysical journey to himself. Most of the young kids who came to the store picked up his books and flicked through them, impressed with his art. They admired his vision and his scope.

Feng did, too. Russell spent hours working on his art. The kids found him an interesting guy and were fascinated by his theory of there being forty-one shades of gray, but lost interest in his storyline. Feng read the comic books as they came out, trying to understand Russell's happiness. Feng wished some of that for himself. As far as he could make out, Russell was happy on the surface, but his sense of isolation was deeply imbedded in the pages of Shades of Gray.

"Wait for me, I'm coming with you," Feng said. Russell must have been in a good mood. He nodded and sat on the bed sketching in his leather-bound book of parchment paper as Feng showered and cleaned his teeth. He looked at his face in the mirror. He missed dreaming and longed to return to . . . something feather-light flickered across his skin.

He turned around, his entire body alight.

For him.

Feng missed him so much. Whoever the hell he was . . .

About the Authors

A.J. Llewellyn lives in California, but dreams of living in Hawaii. Frequent trips to all the islands, bags of Kona coffee in his fridge and a healthy collection of Hawaiian records keep this writer refueled. A.J. loves male/male erotica, has a passion for all animals—especially the dog, the cat and the turtle. A.J. believes that love is a song best sung out loud.

To find out more about A. J., visit www.ajllewellyn.com or you can email her at AJ@AJLlewellyn.com.

D.J. Manly says, "I write not only for my own pleasure, but for the pleasure of my readers. I can't remember a time in my life when I haven't written and told stories. When I'm not writing, I'm dreaming about writing, doing something wild and adventurous, or trying to make the world a better and more open-minded place to live in. I adore beautiful men, and I know I'm not alone in this! Eroticism between consenting adults, in all its many forms, is the icing on the cake of life!"

To find out more about D. J., visit the author's website at http://www.djmanly.com.

www.ingramcontent.com/pod-product-compliance
Lightning Source LLC
LaVergne TN
LVHW020656100826
845148LV00012B/2516
* 9 7 8 1 4 8 7 4 3 1 9 7 6 *